ALSO BY HANNAH McCOUCH

Girl Cook

MOUNTAIN BETTY

Ⓥ VILLARD BOOKS NEW YORK

MOUNTAIN BETTY

a novel

HANNAH McCOUCH

LIBRARY OF CONGRESS CATALOGING-IN-PUBLICATION DATA

McCouch, Hannah.
    Mountain Betty: a novel / Hannah McCouch.
        p. cm.
    ISBN 1-4000-6043-5
    1. Jackson Hole (Wyo.)—Fiction. 2. Ski resorts—Fiction. I. Title.

PS3613.C383M68 2005   2004055489

Villard Books website address: www.villard.com

Printed in the United States of America on acid-free paper

987654321

First Edition

Book design by JoAnne Metsch

For Margaret

MOUNTAIN BETTY

Where I want to start is back around Christmas. I was living with my boyfriend, Jack, in a log cabin at the convergence of the Snake and Hoback rivers. It was our very own miniversion of *True Romance*. The kind that's too impossible to last forever. That's why that movie's so great. The happy ending. It kind of tricks you into believing that two people could go through all of that crap and come out living like millionaires with their adorable baby on a beach in South America somewhere. That's never how it happens in real life though. Not to be too much of a bummer. But seriously, you can only kid yourself for so long.

The cabin was right off Highway 89. Which wasn't a highway in the usual sense—it was no four-laner, more a regular old road. You could see a bridge out the kitchen window that looked like a Roman aqueduct. In Manhattan, a view of that bridge would command serious bucks. But this one didn't have the same cachet as a view of, say, the *Brooklyn* Bridge. In Hoback Junction, getting away from things like bridges was the whole point. I don't want you thinking we were living large or anything.

Anyway, the cabin was pretty much a one-room deal, with a separate kitchen and a bathroom the size of a postage stamp. It had a propane stove and a big stone fireplace that leaked cool breezes even when the flue was closed. The bulbous pink fifties refrigerator with the stainless pull handle was my favorite thing about the place.

Not that it wasn't quaint. Just a little dark since Jack had stapled plastic on the windows to keep the drafts down. So you could call it rustic, or you could call it depressing, depending on your mood. In fact, depending on whether you were being honest with yourself on any given day, you could call the place a trailer, with logs stuck on the outside to make it look all Davy Crockett. It was part of a cluster of fishing cabins down on the point. Each one had a name—Lodge, Pinyon, Pinecone—very sweet. Fishermen apparently rented them weekly for mucho dinero in the summertime. Or so Jim, the new owner, said. In the winter he could give us a deal because Hoback was twelve miles south of the town of Jackson, and about twenty-five miles from Teton Village, where the ski area was, so it was a bit of a haul.

I should probably clarify the whole "Jackson Hole" thing. Whenever I refer to it as Jackson, people always say, "You mean, Jackson *Hole*?" Like perhaps I'm not saying it right. It confused me a little at first too. The "Hole," as it was explained to me, refers to the entire valley, encompassing what I guess you could call the "villages" or "towns" of Jackson town center, Kelly, Moose, Wilson, and Teton Village, each with its own post office. And most locals don't call it "Jackson Hole" in casual parlance, just "Jackson." So now you know.

Jack and I moved in together at the beginning of October and we didn't have a phone, so calls were made on the pay phone up the hill at the Hoback Motel, the money-losing arm of Jim's real estate empire. It wasn't hard to see why. The place was kind of Bates-like, truth be told.

But Jim was pretty cool. Nice, the way midwesterners can be. He'd moved with his wife, Cathy, and their two kids from Ohio or Kansas or somewhere. If you ask me, the guy had his work cut out for him. There wasn't much going on down there in Hoback. I'm sure he'd made his purchase with an eye toward the future though. In a few years it'll probably be hot, like Jackson, and the only people able to afford it will be the rich. Jim said if we ever had friends come to visit, they could stay up at the motel for cheap. Ten dollars a night or something ridiculous. That's the kind of guy he was. So the place could be seen as creepy to the naked eye. But to me, on most days, it felt like home.

We'd cut the wood that was stacked on the porch ourselves. Boy, did that make me feel mountainy. Driving up into the hills in Jack's Chevy Silverado, hauling out dead trees like a pair of friggin' lumberjacks. Jack had taught me how to use the chain saw, and the ax. The most important thing to remember about chopping wood, he said, was keeping your legs wide apart when bringing the ax down so as not to lodge the blade in your kneecap. I kept forgetting though, and almost did myself a couple of times. It was pretty hair-raising. Not as hair-raising as the chain saw part by a long shot. The whole procedure was in descending order of fear. The hair went up with the chain saw. Then came back down a little when you got to the ax.

I liked being seen as the sort of girl who could wield those appliances with a certain amount of authority. Even if I was secretly about to shit a ten-pound brick. I'd have that chain saw cranking, the reverberations shooting through my body like electroshock therapy, and all I could think was, I had no business, no business whatsoever, handling one of those things.

Every once in a while you'd hear gruesome stories about chain saws "kicking back" into the jugulars of real he-men—men who pulled those cords every day of the week. If those guys were getting aced, what sort of chance would a sissy girl like me have? I'm not saying I can't be macho when the situation calls for it. But fear is a pretty crippling thing. And clearly, when it came to chain saws, Fear was my middle name.

But that's the way things were with Jack—danger masquerading as normalcy, if that makes any sense. The kind of stuff you hear about in the news—accidents where you can't quite believe people would be so stupid. Except I can, because I was.

chapter 2

I'd moved to Alta, Utah, from New York City the *previous* Christmas, after getting fired from a small video production company that did industrials for my father's law firm. The boss, Lieberman, was eager to suck up to Dad, and I was eager to suck up to anyone who'd give me a job. They hired me the summer after I graduated from a small liberal arts college upstate, and everyone was pleased as punch. The whole thing went exactly as planned from the point of view of postcollegiate success stories. That is, get hooked with an internship and work your way up from the bottom. It looked like my career had officially begun.

Lieberman was a high-strung guy who paced the halls clapping his hands, yelling things like "Come on, come on, come on! Let's get cracking!" As if we weren't all busting our humps to begin with. As far as I could tell, the only person *not* cracking was him.

But that's neither here nor there. As a lackey, I had the job of writing and producing the "Didja Know?" segment for this food show that ran on cable. I'd hang out at big touristy inter-sections like Fifty-ninth Street where the Plaza meets the Park, with a cameraman and a sound guy eliciting reactions to gems like "Did you know that back in the dark ages people ate with spoons because the fork was considered the devil's instru-ment?" Stuff like that. People stopped and talked to me too. Not to pat myself on the back or anything, but I was all right at my job.

Things started falling apart when the food show ended and Lieberman asked me to make sales calls. I just couldn't get on board. Especially if it was going to benefit that jerk Lieber-man. Making those calls was so painful that I began faking it—having in-depth conversations with the dial tone whenever I heard him clapping down the hall.

It was around this time that Lieberman called me into his of-fice. The way he was pacing back and forth, running his hand angrily through his winged, prematurely graying hair, I knew I was about to get chewed out for *something*. Lieberman was prone to throwing tantrums for the hell of it, so we could all see what a creative and passionate individual he was.

There was a styrofoam cup sitting in the middle of his desk, a lipstick smudge on the rim, remnants of stale Cremoraed cof-fee festering in its depths. The vein in Lieberman's temple was about to erupt. Pointing to the cup, he said, "I found *that* in the editing room."

I didn't know exactly what he was getting at so I said, "Uh-huh."

"Don't you 'uh-huh' me, Winters! I've got your number!"

I'd seen him go off before, but never like this. The man was unhinged.

"Do you think this office is your *fucking* trash can? Huh? *Huh?* HUH!" He stood there, mustache twitching.

His reaction seemed so totally out of proportion to the crime that I thought he might be pulling a Candid Camera on me or something. I didn't want to seem foolish, so I cracked a smile.

Bad move. Before I knew it, his face was in mine. He said, "You better wipe that smile off your face and give me some goddamn answers here or I swear . . ."

The spit was flying. I'd stopped smiling. Indeed, I was so flustered, I had no answers for anything. A leathery lump gathered in my throat, and I must have looked like I was having a hard time swallowing, because Lieberman's face slackened somewhat. An indicator, he must have thought. Proof. It didn't take long to work myself up into a full-blown crying jag. Now that I think of it, that's probably why bullies get such a kick out of me. Maximum tear return.

When I was finally able to speak, I denied any knowledge of said cup and astutely pointed out that I didn't wear lipstick. Besides which, I managed to add, I wasn't a slob. I'm extremely anal when it comes to stuff like that. It didn't matter though. Lieberman had already made up his mind. In fact, it occurred to me on more than one occasion that he'd made up the entire scenario just so he'd have an excuse to fire me.

After that, I went into panic mode. December in New York

City is no time to be without a job. You can get pretty suicidal walking around amidst the glittery white lights on Madison Avenue when you don't have a dime to your name.

Through a help wanted ad in the *Times*, I got a part-time gig. Unlike the Salvation Army Santas, ringing their bells and jingling their change cups outside Bloomingdale's, I was stationed, wearing four-inch stilettos and an enormous rare mink, on the sidewalk outside the Trump Plaza. Perched beside me was a huge cardboard sign that said, PRESTIGE FURS. If you consider loitering in the freezing cold for hours with your toes jammed into unnatural positions easy, aside from getting generally harassed and spit on a couple of times, you might say it was pretty easy money.

That's approximately where I was at seven months after receiving my diploma, when the Winters clan headed out to the Buckeye Lodge in Alta, for our annual Christmas holiday. To my parents' consternation, I wound up staying. The idea was, take a couple of months off from the New York rat race to mull the future over while waiting tables and brushing up on my ski technique. Sounds legit enough, no?

The Buckeye was a regular Peyton Place. The vodka flowed like wine, the 3.2 beer tasted like water . . . The scent of burning cannabis was so prevalent the management might as well have been pumping it in through the vents. As for the "snow," let's just say we were living on a dirt road at the end of Little Cottonwood Canyon, but it felt like *Bright Lights, Big City* to us. It was the perfect spot to be a delinquent if that was what you were into. And let me just say, I *was*.

chapter 3

The snow was coming down hard, and I was out near the parking area splitting wood with my legs so far apart that my groin hurt, when Jim came down from the office and told me I had a call. The only people who ever called on that pay phone were my parents and Jack's wife. Oh yeah. He was married. There were complications.

It was dark, around seven o'clock, and I had the night off while Jack worked the fryolator at the Mangy Moose. We'd have wings and nachos for dinner when he got home. Jim was wearing his Elmer Fudd hat, which I'd liked so much that Jack had gone out and bought me my very own red plaid, earflapped version with a pom-pom on top. Jack was sweet that way. And generous. The problem was, he never had any money, so his generosity had limits.

"Hey, nice hat." It's what Jim always said when he saw me wearing it.

"Not as nice as yours" was my standard reply.

"Lady on the phone forya. No accent."

That meant it wasn't Jack's wife. She was French. We'd explained the situation to Jim after Muriel called making various threats. She lived down in Salt Lake, and they were separated, but still. The French thing was something I used in order to rationalize some of the crazy shit she said. Not that she didn't have her reasons.

"You want me to tell her you're not here?"

"No, it's okay," I said, taking my time up the steep, icy drive, looking for bits of sand to grip onto. The phone conversations I'd been having with my parents lately were nothing to rush into.

A dull yellow light hung above the phone next to the door that said "Office." That's where Jim and his family lived.

"Hello?"

"Hello, sweetheart, how are you?" It was Mom. And forced enthusiasm was the word.

An uncomfortable lull pretty much put the kibosh on that.

"Elizabeth? Are you there?"

"Yeah, I'm here," I said, smashing a snowy ice ball with the toe of my Sorel.

"How are you feeling?"

"Fine," I said, wondering what the last ailment I'd mentioned was.

"Didn't you have a cold?"

"Oh, right. That's gone now." I'd resorted to inventing various illnesses over the past several months in an attempt to raise my parents' sympathy. Otherwise our communication was barely what you'd call communication at all. They'd taken on a letter writing campaign in the hopes that their fears concerning what I *wasn't* doing with my life would be better conveyed.

"I'm so glad. Did you take my advice about the vitamin C? A thousand milligrams?"

"I did." Not true. Those vitamins were way too expensive.

"Keep taking it. You don't want it to come back. I've been getting terrible sinus infections, myself."

I'll take your cold, and raise you a sinus infection.

"Sinus infection, how did you get that?" Our maladies enabled us to commiserate in ways we never could as healthy human beings.

"The doctor says it could be from a molar I had a root canal on two years ago. *Two* root canals actually. *That tooth.* It's cost me quite a pretty penny."

"I'll bet," I said, thinking I damn well better not run into any tooth trouble. It would be the old yarn and yank for me. "That doesn't sound good."

"How's your skin, by the way?"

"My skin?" *What had I told her about my skin?*

"The eczema's clearing up?"

"Oh. The eczema. Right. Not too bad right now."

"You're *sure* it's eczema? You've been to a doctor?"

"Of course." I wasn't about to tell her I didn't have any health insurance. That would push her over the edge.

"And the doctor said *eczema*?"

Just so you know, this was code for "You don't have AIDS, do you?"

"That's what the doctor said."

"Oh, thank God." She breathed a sigh of relief.

I waited for her to get to the point. There was always a point.

"So Daddy and I have been thinking."

Oh brother. When those two started thinking, clear the decks.

"We'd like to come out there for a little visit. Doesn't that sound like fun?"

"A blast."

"I don't like your tone."

Here we go. "I'm sorry, Mom. That sounds great. Really. When are you coming?" The truth was, I was kind of excited by the prospect of seeing them. Having a nice meal or two. I was getting sick of wings and nachos.

"We thought we'd come out for Christmas. Do a little skiing."

"Awesome," I said, trying to sound upbeat. The longer the hitch took to come, the more hopeful I became. "You could probably get a room right here at the motel."

"Don't be silly, dear. We're not going to stay in a *motel*. I've got reservations for us at the Spring Creek Ranch. . . . There's just one thing."

I knew it.

"We only want to see *you*."

"What do you mean, you only want to see *me*?"

"I mean, we don't *condone* your *living situation*."

Finally. The Point.

"Benny's coming. The hotel restaurant is supposed to be lovely."

My younger brother, Benny, was still in college and hadn't done anything to piss them off yet. I was going on my second season as a ski bum and wasn't exactly doing them proud in the life advancement department. It made them angry. And worried. And their anger and worry worried and angered me. It was an unhealthy situation all around. "That's bullshit," I said.

"I'm not going to discuss this any further if you continue using that sort of language."

"Look, Mom. I'm not a kid anymore. I'd like to see you, I really would, but you're putting me in a bad position here."

"*We're* putting *you* in a bad position?" She managed to stifle the contemptuous laughter.

As usual, things were degenerating.

Jack's truck swung into the lot, and I felt a momentary surge of relief. We had our life. We'd take them on. "Look, maybe we could ski—"

"Did he even graduate *high* school? *You* tell *me*. Never mind that he's still married."

"He graduated high school," I said quietly.

"Okay, college. What about *college*?"

"What about it? Not everyone goes to college, you know. He's skilled at other things. Things you don't learn in school."

"Like what? Cheating on his poor wife?"

Actually, I'd been thinking of the time he'd winched a friend's truck out of a riverbed, but that wasn't the sort of thing she was likely to appreciate. "He's separated," I wanted to say. But why bother? I breathed deeply and kept my mouth shut.

Jack rolled down his window and gave me an inquiring look. God, he was spectacular. Those big green eyes, the velvety, honey blond hair, the chiseled jaw.

"You all right?" he asked quietly.

Why couldn't they just leave us alone? It would have made life so much easier. "Fine," I mouthed.

"Mom? You there?"

A quiet, deceptively nonchalant "I'm here."

"I've gotta go now."

"You may not think so now," she said ominously, "but *one day* you might just miss me." Invoking the specter of death had been Mom's ace in the hole ever since I could remember.

"Why, are you going somewhere?" This time, I wasn't falling for it.

"I'm just saying," she said, pushing the envelope, "those lumps in my breast were benign, thank God, but no one lives forever."

There'd been a recent cancer scare.

"Well, you're okay for now, right?"

"The stress you're putting us under hasn't exactly been *rejuvenating*," she said, breathing out dramatically.

"Maybe you need a massage?" I offered. It was a joke. Mom never went in for things like massages. As far as I could tell, she was *into* stress. I was just trying to lighten her up.

"Oh, give me a break." I could hear her blowing her nose in the background. Was she crying? I really hated it when she cried. And come to think of it, she probably knew that.

"When are you planning on coming?" I asked, attempting to divert her.

"Christmas." She sighed.

"Christmas Day?"

"Christmas Eve."

"Well, I'll look forward to it," I said. Sometimes changing the subject was the only decent option.

"So will we."

And occasionally it worked.

After the phone call with Mom, I sat on the porch in the cold for a while, glad I had long johns on under my jeans. Staring up at the silhouette of mountains beyond the highway, I thought about how much bigger they were than my stupid little problems. That made me feel better. To think about nature, even God maybe, and how things would keep going on regardless of all my petty bullshit. How long, I wondered, would I be able to last if I headed out into the wilderness right now? With no food, water, or extra clothing . . .

Nothing like putting things into perspective.

The smell of hot sauce seared my nostrils as I entered the kitchen. Jack had stuck the wings and nachos in the oven to warm while he took a shower. In the main room, a fire was blazing.

Extracting the wet liners from my gloves, I placed them decoratively in front of the fire, far enough from the flame so they wouldn't melt. I took off my damp socks and did the same, draping the rest of my clothes on the armchair. Jack would give me a hard time about that later. It was one of the worst habits I had, draping clothes on chairs.

The bathroom was so small you could practically be on the toilet and in the shower at the same time. Opening and closing the door quickly so as not to let the steam escape, I pushed the curtain aside and climbed in.

Jack took me in his warm, wet arms. "You ready to get pelted?" he asked, placing me under the pins and needles of the acupuncture-like spray, rubbing his hands up and down the sides of me. "You're freezing."

I didn't want to spoil his good mood, so I tried to get Zen about the steamy warmth of the shower, the sweet sensation of Jack's hands on my skin as he worked up an Irish Spring lather, soaping me from head to toe. "You're clean," he finally said. With his hands on my waist, he moved in close from behind, sealing his body against mine. "Ouch. Goddamnit."

"What?"

"I got nailed in the eye."

So much for the power of positive thinking.

"I'm gonna shave. I want my face to be *silky* smooth," he said, leering as he moved the curtain aside with a flourish.

Jack's face was always soft. He had the kind of facial hair that barely grew, and when it did, it came out sort of soft and peach fuzzy, like that of a kid who hadn't started shaving yet.

Through the clear map-of-the-world shower curtain, as I let the water pelt the cream rinse right out of my hair, I watched him shaving naked in a pair of Adidas slides with the rubber nodules on the soles. *Meticulous* could have been Jack's middle name, I swear. You'd never catch him messing up a pair of socks on that dusty wall-to-wall. Not that he was a germ freak.

I almost saw his whole aesthetic as being slightly, I don't know, Scandinavian or something.

Closing my eyes, I tried to get back into the zone. I didn't want to get out until I'd completely thawed. Sometimes, the shower is the only place where you can really let your mind go blank and just be one with the moment, you know?

I guess I'm pretty keyed up most of the time, because even when I'm supposed to be relaxing in the shower, I'm worrying about stuff. Like that phone conversation with Mom. Or the fact that I was going to have to work seventeen hours the next day.

Jack had warmed up the sheets, strategically placing the Neutrogena sesame after-shower oil I'd recently blown a serious wad on on the bedside table. The room was warm by the fire, cooler by the bed. I kept the towel wrapped around my shoulders, letting it slide to the floor at the last minute.

"Wait," Jack said, pushing me back, "I want to look at you."

I stood where I was a few seconds, drinking in the rapt expression on his face. "Jack, it's cold." I was getting chilled and a little self-conscious.

"Comeer," he drawled, flipping open the comforter.

chapter **4**

I think I fell in love with Jack the day we almost died together. I know it sounds melodramatic, but you really had to be there. It was back in Alta, where we'd met working at the Buckeye. Jack had just snaked out a toilet in one of the suites, and I was in between breakfast and dinner shifts when we decided to climb and ski Flagstaff, the mountain across the street from the lodge that served as a playground for the snowboarders who weren't allowed on Alta Mountain.

It was afternoon, and we were doing some bushwhacking. Which, by definition, is not the smartest thing to do. Ever. But anyway. We'd diverted from the main path and I could make the excuse that we were following *someone's* tracks, just not the right ones. The route had started out reasonably enough, looking like a more direct line to the top. But appearances in these instances are often misleading. The higher we climbed, the hairier things got, and soon we were scrambling up rock crevasses, clasping onto tiny, curled trees.

Jack had lent me his extra shell and bibs so I wasn't in my usual *Saturday Night Fever* throwback wear—ellesse stretchies and a corduroy CB jacket. He'd started lending me things from the moment we met—Ray-Ban glacier glasses, Grandoe gloves, Bollé goggles. I saw it almost as a form of courtship. I was a bit of an Eliza Doolittle when I first got out west. Anyway, no one could say we weren't *dressed* for success.

Jack stopped at the base of several boulders where the tracks went off in all directions. Taking off his pack he surveyed the rocks, which were big, steep, and icy, and said, "Follow me."

And I did, step for clunky step. Downhill ski boots *have* no traction, so it wasn't like climbing in hiking boots with Vibram treads, more like those weird, castlike shoes Herman Munster wore. When things got really dicey, Jack would reach back and offer his hand.

At the top of the rock face was a large tree, whose thick, gray trunk would have to be skirted in order for us to continue. It had to have been over four feet wide. Getting around it would require serious gymnastics. I've always sucked at gymnastics.

Sticking his boot out, Jack stomped the ledge several times to see if it would hold, while I stared at the trunk of the tree, psyching myself out thinking, *There's no way, there's no way, there's no way.* In the greatest Fear Fantasy I'm ever likely to indulge in, I envisioned us smashing into rocks, suffocating on snow, experiencing agonizing pain in ways no one ever wants to think about when they're a tightrope away from safety.

If Jack was as scared as I was, he wasn't showing it. Looking at me confidently, he said, "Watch me and do what I do. I'm going to spread my arms out and hug the trunk as hard as I can. You want to position your boots on the ledge so your toes are pointing out, like a ballet dancer's. See? Look at my legs. Like that," he said.

I didn't want to look down at his legs because then I would see how far there was to fall.

"Betty," he said, grabbing my chin, "look at my legs. Like that, got it? When I get to the other side, you're going to go. There's nothing to be scared of. I'll be right there to catch you if you fall. Take off your pack. I'm throwing them across."

It all happened so fast there was hardly any time to think of dying, which is how I think a lot of people wind up dead in these circumstances.

Jack straddled and gripped the gray trunk, smoothly, quickly, his whole body pressed up against it, legs and toes like a ballerina's in second position. He stood there for a beat and speedily moved on to the other side, where he breathed out a short, adrenaline-pumped breath.

"Okay. Nothing to be scared of," he said, "it's easy. You can do it. I'm right here."

"Easy for you to say." My heart ricocheted. "The trunk's too wide. I don't think my arms will reach." If I'd been a little calmer, I might have really started to whine.

"Nonsense. Don't stand there psyching yourself out. Go for it! Make your move! Do it! Now!"

I didn't have much of a choice. Going back down the way we'd come wasn't a less dangerous proposition. Taking a few quick breaths, I thrust out my right arm and gripped the tree. I stood that way, every muscle and fiber of my being tensed, for what felt like minutes, thinking, *If I don't move, nothing bad can happen.*

"Good! You're good!" Jack's voice ripped through my reverie. "Now reach your hand over and I'll grab you."

I looked over at Jack. Would he be able to hold me if I fell? Between a cliff and a hard place, I had no choice but to trust him. Inching my left boot around closer to the right, I prepared to make my move. Leaping sideways, I felt Jack's hand on my elbow, the two of us falling together into the soft snow on the other side.

I could have blamed Jack for getting me into that spot to begin with. He'd been living in Alta for years and knew what we were doing was dangerous and more than a little stupid. In a way, I knew it too. But it felt so good to be alive. And falling in love. So instead of blaming him, I thanked him for saving my life.

Sitting at the top of Flagstaff smoking a ceremonial joint, eating the requisite Granny Smith apple, staring out at the pink-purple clouds as the sun shined through the jagged peaks of the Wasatch, a hawk circling low in the sky. . . . I knew then and there that the whole crazy adventure was everything I'd come west to experience.

* * *

We popped up some corn, sprinkled it with salt and Tabasco, and settled on the scruffy couch to watch snowy reruns of *Cheers*. To get even two channels on our crappy black-and-white TV required serious antennae futzing and bits of aluminum foil. Jack had stopped off at Albertson's to pick up some Old Style, a watery midwestern brew he swore by. Mostly, because it was cheap—six something, for a twelver.

"Popcorn," Jack said, his legs propped on the coffee table next to the TV, "nature's perfect snack." He had all of these low-fat snacking tricks for his bike racing. Come February he'd put himself on a diet (which had more to do with curtailing the beer and pot than it did with losing weight) and start training.

The Tabasco stung as we dug our fingers into the popcorn in the stainless mixing bowl on Jack's lap. *Cheers* wasn't really my favorite show or anything, but it's amazing how attached you can get to a program when it's the only thing on. "My parents want to come for a visit," I said.

Jack arched an eyebrow. "You're kidding."

"Nope."

"That's great, Betty," he said, thinking, as I had, that they'd finally come around.

He was killing me, he really was. He had this thing, maybe it was innocence or sensitivity or something, that just made you want to hurt yourself when you upset him.

"Yeah," I said, pausing. I didn't have the heart to bring up the inevitable. Jack had met my mother briefly back in Alta, and she'd made him feel like a world-class turkey. I'd told him she did that with everyone.

Still, he'd said, "I'm not smart enough for you, Betty."

My friends from home would have had a good laugh over *that*. I think he felt sort of less-than because he *hadn't* gone to college. I also think he had a learning disability that no one ever addressed when he was growing up. The only reason I'd clued in was from the letters he'd written to me over the summer that had a bunch of weird spelling mistakes with letters upside down and backward. The sad thing was, it made him hate school, and reading. You could tell that he was innately a smart person, that if only he'd been handled correctly, he wouldn't have had to spend the rest of his life feeling like such an idiot.

The irony was, he could ski and bike the pants off just about anyone. He was disciplined, and strong, and he excelled. That's what I admired about him. I could honestly say I'd never met anyone like Jack. Who's to say some dork is better, just because he's a college grad? Half the guys in my class were bigger fuckups than most ski bums I knew. Actually, most of the ski bums I knew *were* college grads.

As far as I could tell, when it came to my mother, *no* one was ever good enough for me. I'm not saying that's not a natural way for a mother to feel. It did make dating pretty tough though. And having friends in general. It seemed like the more I liked someone, the more critical she became. And her judgment about people was lousy. The few she approved of were the ones who looked all spiffy on the outside but who could have made the short list of the biggest degenerates of all time.

Maybe that's not so natural, who can say? I don't have anything else to compare it to. It didn't give me too much confidence about my choices in life, that's for sure.

Anyway, where was I? Oh yeah, the couch.

I said, "They only want to see *me*."

"What do you mean, they only want to see *you*?" he asked, pausing on a mouthful of popcorn.

"They don't want to condone our relationship." I didn't bother holding up my fingers in quotes around the word "condone." Jack didn't really appreciate stuff like that.

He took another handful of popcorn and chewed. After about three minutes he said, "You told them no I hope."

Staring at my beer, I said, "Not exactly."

"Betty."

"What?"

"Why do you always cave in to them?"

"They're my parents?"

"Yeah, so, they should respect your choices."

"You're married."

"Separated. And I'll be getting divorced as soon as Muriel gets her papers. We've been through all this."

It was a sore topic. In fact, he was going to have to take a trip down to Salt Lake soon to prove to a judge that he and Muriel were *still* happily married. Guilt kept me from bitching. I was just the girlfriend. She was his wife. Jack was the one that wanted the separation in the first place. He wasn't going to screw her on her chances for citizenship. That was part of the deal. So he'd do what he had to do. It was only right.

"They've gotta stop treating you like a kid."

"Tell me about it."

"Well, they're not staying here."

"No."

"Because Gibby is coming up."

"Gibby's coming up?" This was a very unwelcome bit of news. "When were you going to tell me about *that*?"

"I just got a postcard today. It's okay if he stays here, right?"

"Where's he going to sleep?"

"Sleeping bag."

The thing was, we'd had this discussion about visitors before. Jack knew I didn't want a bunch of Alta ski bums using our place as a crash pad.

"On the floor. Or the couch."

"Maybe he could stay up at the motel?"

"He's a friend, Betty, he's coming to stay with us. I'm not going to ask him to stay at the motel."

"How long's he coming for?"

"Just the weekend. What's up with you anyway? I thought you liked Gibby."

"I do," I said, sucking the salt off my fingers and wiping them on a used tissue.

Gibby was a big bear of a guy whose hyena laugh was distinguishable in even the most crowded of bars. But his primary function up in Alta, besides regaling people with tall tales and his day job as a lifty, was to supply the entire community with more coke than they could possibly snort or, in most cases, afford. He was a decent guy. As far as drug deal-

ers go. Which isn't saying much. Jack had been on his best behavior since we'd moved up here, and I wanted to keep it that
way.

"Where you going?"

"Brush my teeth."

"Betty."

"Yeah?"

"What's wrong?"

"Nothing."

The scent of freshly brewing coffee filled the cabin. Jack was in the kitchen cooking up eggs, bacon, and toast in his instructor's sweater and bibs. A bong sat like a candle on the kitchen table between two place settings. There was a Grateful Dead Steal Your Face skull stuck onto the red plastic. I think one of the guys from the Buckeye snuck it on there. Because Jack wasn't exactly what you'd call a fan. I wasn't really a Deadhead myself, although I did enjoy the odd "Sugar Magnolia." It made me nostalgic for college.

"Hope you're hungry," he said, turning with the spatula to give me a good-morning kiss.

I was never very hungry in the morning and Jack knew it, but like a mother who's not going to let her kid leave for school on an empty stomach, he would cook me breakfast and I would damn well eat it. "I'll go warm up the truck," I said, hoping the walk and biting morning air would give me an appetite.

"Already did that. Sit down and eat." There was a small window next to the pink fridge that wasn't covered by plastic and looked out onto barren aspens and the Snake River below. Through it, I tried to gauge the weather.

"It's twenty below," he said. "Supposed to warm up by noon though. You better wear an extra pair of long johns."

I had to admit, I liked Jack's maternal side. I'd never had a boyfriend care so much about my well-being.

The drug thing we could overcome.

Jack pulled out a Classico spaghetti jar filled with buds from a plant he'd grown in his tiny backyard in Salt Lake. There were six more jars just like it in the cupboard. When he cracked the top, the aroma of skunk weed trumped those of the coffee and bacon. Snapping a piece off a pineconelike cluster, Jack packed the bowl.

"When was the last time you changed the water in that thing?" I asked, pouring myself a cup of coffee. I was trying to subtly call attention to how much pot we were smoking. At the start of my western odyssey, being able to spark up wherever, whenever, felt like this great antiestablishment fuck the world. A year later, I was getting a little sick of it if you want to know the truth. The wake and bake had me worried.

"This'll give you an appetite," he said, sealing his thumb over the tiny hole and flaming the bowl with a Bic. Inhaling half the smoke in the tube, he covered the top with his hand and held it out to me.

"No thanks," I said. And not because I was above such

things either. It was a matter of pacing. I'd probably light up as soon as we hit the quad later that day.

"Sure?" he frogged, managing to hold most of the smoke in.

He waited for me to say "Yeah" before exhaling and breathing in the rest, letting it out slowly as he doled the food onto two plastic camping plates. The toast was already buttered. I love it when people butter your toast. It's the ultimate act of kindness.

"You want OJ?"

"Yes, please," I said, staring down at the food on my plate, wishing I was hungry. It's not that I'm finicky, or don't have an appetite in general, just not at six-thirty in the morning. For me, those pangs don't usually kick in until at least ten. By that time, we'd be out on the slopes working. I'd be starved by lunch whether I ate breakfast or not. "How about tuna today?" I asked.

"Bread gets too soggy."

"PB and J?"

"How about we use up that leftover chicken in the fridge?"

I made a mean leftover chicken-and-pickle sandwich. The pickles were one of my mother's trademarks. Those bologna and Wonder bread kids at school used to tease me until they got a taste of the secret ingredient. Then everyone wanted to trade.

My ruby red, cat-eye Vuarnets hung from Croakies around Jack's neck. He was totally comfortable wearing a pair of ladies' sunglasses. It fit into his alternative aesthetic—the White Stripes, the Chemical Brothers, the Strokes, and my girl-friend's sunglasses, right *on*.

Before either of us could answer the knock at the door, our neighbor Speed was standing in the middle of the kitchen, doing a modified John Belushi, *Animal House* ninja man, until his eyes focused on the bong. "Amigos."

"Help yourself, Speed," Jack said.

Speed's real name was Harlin Babcock, but no one ever called him that. He was older than us, in his early thirties. At first I felt silly calling him Speed. Then I realized he really dug that nickname. He was originally from Tennessee, a Desert Storm vet who worked rentals at Teton Village Sports. People called him Speed because he rode his uniski faster than most people drove.

Speed had only one arm, so I held the bong to his lips while he sparked it with his good hand. I helped more to be gracious than anything else. He was a real wiz with that stump— perfectly capable of lighting up his own bongs. Hell, the guy was a hunter for Christ's sake. If you ever saw him in a dark alley, with his long, scruffy hair sticking up all over the place and his unshaven face, you might start walking a little faster. But like a lot of scary looking dudes, he was actually a real sweetheart. And *scary* can be a pretty subjective word. Because if you ask me, Speed was kind of hot. He was also gentle in this almost childlike way.

It made you wonder what it would take for him to snap. He'd been in the Special Forces. You hear stories, memory suppression and all that, going apeshit out of nowhere . . . He'd had us over for elk barbecues in the fall and kept us in buffalo— ground, rib eyes, tenderloin, and shoulder. Mostly, he was cool about us as a couple, made us feel normal, like he really admired what we had.

It wasn't the kind of support we were used to. Jack's mother had taken Muriel's side when they'd separated. Thought I was some kind of wild, coke-addicted Courtney Love. Probably because that was what Muriel told her. Which was pretty funny. Because as far as I could tell, Muriel was the one with the coke problem.

A little backstory here might be helpful. The reason I'd moved up to Jackson in the spring was to get away from Jack. I didn't want to be the reason his marriage, which was all of a year old, fell apart. Let's just say, I was trying to do the right thing. Albeit, after I'd done some damage.

We spent the spring and most of the summer completely incommunicado. Except for a couple of those hard-to-read letters I mentioned. In the fall, Jack left Muriel and came after me. There was none of this Dr. Joy Browne, "wait a year before moving on to the next relationship" stuff. Not that I think it's bad advice for people with a certain amount of patience and maturity.

No, Jack and I were of the Immediate If Not Sooner School of Gratification. So you might say, the corpse was still warm. Breathing even. We moved in together *before the wound had healed*, as it were.

"You guys catching the first tram this morning?" Speed asked.

"Did it snow last night?" I had to know. I'd turned into sort of a powder snob since moving out west. At the beginning, I could barely even *ski* powder, having learned on the hardpack and blue ice back east. Now it was like, the conditions had to be *champagne*, otherwise I didn't really see the point.

"It's been dust on crust the past couple of days," Speed said, "but I think they got six to twelve on top last night and it's supposed to start up again later today."

"Come on, Betty, get your stuff on," Jack said, heading out to deal with the windshield, which by now was primed—ice warmed and melted—for scraping.

I whipped together the chicken-and-pickle sandwiches, wrapped them in aluminum foil, and threw them in a large brown paper bag with four frozen Toll House cookies, a Nalgene bottle filled with water, and a couple of peach Dannons. Stuffing the bag into my bright yellow North Face backpack, I flung it over one shoulder, slung my boots over the other, and made my way out into the frosty Wyoming morning.

The clouds were scattered, a pale yellow light glowing on one side of the mountains, a low fog hanging over the river. Magpies hopped around on spidery feet, jumping into trees, flying away, circling, landing again. Sometimes, on mornings like that, I'd take in a deep, cold breath and my heart would expand with gratefulness. I know it sounds corny, but there was something about the land that made you feel lucky to be alive and standing, breathing in the cool scent of pine and woodsmoke. A lot of mornings were like that in Jackson. It made you want to get up early so as not to miss them. It was 7:00 A.M., and as I sat shotgun in Jack's truck taking in the snowcapped buttes, with Neil Young's pinched-nose voice singing "Sugar Mountain" and an EMS travel mug cupped in my hands, I thought, *It doesn't get any better than this.*

chapter 6

The usual suspects lined up for the first tram early that morning. Season passes were pulled out from underneath sweaters and prominently displayed. Poles were leaned on, heels of boots thrust forward to take the load off and give a little stretch. Some held paper cups of coffee from the Bear Claw, the warm aroma mingling with clouds of steamy breath. Speed cleared his throat, burped, and farted. Jack answered in kind. Speed said, "Betty, wouldya knock it off?"

I smiled and winked at him. It was all part of the ritual. The after-dawn serenade. It wouldn't be a morning in Jackson if someone wasn't burping or farting, and we all knew it.

I had a few things on my mind. Like whether the privilege of being on the first tram that morning was worth the twenty-five (sometimes less) bucks I made each day as a ski instructor. I'd been tipped only once so far that season. Ten bucks. Which, believe it or not, I was elated to have. That's where I was at financially. I'd pretty much blown through my graduation money, which I should point out, wasn't a king's ransom or anything. The used Subaru had eaten up most of it. Then there were a new pair of Lange boots, a shell, bibs, a pile jacket, and some used telemark gear. Now I was down to, like, zero. Jack wasn't faring much better. He'd gone into credit card debt when he left his job at the Buckeye in the fall. Things were getting tight.

I *was* on line for the first tram though, so I tried to look on the bright side. I thought of all of my friends, sitting in cubicles back in New York City. Unlike them, I was dressed comfortably in highly breathable materials and was about to hit Rendezvous Bowl. I knew they would be jealous. But it had started occurring to me more and more lately that skiing had been a lot more fun when I was doing it on vacation. I didn't want to cocktail waitress and ski instruct the rest of my life, but the whole question of what it was I *did* want to do was pretty damn murky. Which put a damper on the whole ski bum thing insofar as *joy* was concerned.

I don't know how it was possible to graduate from four years of liberal arts and not have a clue. I mean, I wound up doing okay in school, but that whole question about what you're going to *do* with the rest of your life . . . I'd thought a little freewheelin' fun time would do the trick. Back then I'd figured, if I didn't do some oat sowing, I'd sit in an office, get married, have kids, and die a slow death. Somewhere in between mule kicks, three sixties, bong hits, and back scratchers, there had to be an answer to who I was and what I was cut out for in this world. It would dawn slowly, in a mind unfettered by material and societal constraints. I know some people don't have the luxury to debate this question, but it seemed that I did.

When you're twenty-one, people expect you to know what's what. Your parents for instance. Especially after they've dropped wads of cash on your hoity-toity private education . . . *Screwed* is the only word for it. At least, I could see how they would see it this way. I blame the system. I mean, who the hell knows what she wants to do with her life when she's twenty-one? Not me, that's for damn sure.

Okay. That's not completely true. I was a comp. lit. major. I'd gotten an A in an incredibly demanding film class. I know that doesn't exactly sound legit, but some of the film classes I've taken . . . I mean, you think they're going to be gut, like you're going to kick back with a few football players, watch a flick or two, and chew the fat awhile. Then you find yourself discussing the Heimlich and Un-Heimlich aspects of *The Texas Chain Saw Massacre*. Which, I'm sorry, but I'd always thought, shitty slasher flick. Little did I know. There are people in this world that make their living out of dissecting, theorizing, psychoanalyzing, and generally making totally impenetrable *The Texas Chain Saw Massacre*.

All that just to say, when I graduated I thought I wanted to move out to L.A. and make films. And you know what? I got talked out of it. This isn't going to be some kind of blame-the-parents tale either. Not to worry. But you know if I had to think about why I made certain decisions in my life, well, there was some influence from the old parental peanut gallery, that's for sure. Don't ask me why I was such a goddamn pushover. Parents, man, they're a trip. Sometimes I don't think they even know how much power they have.

You see my mother, who'd barely ever even been to L.A., harbored this weird, almost postapocalyptic vision of it. She (and my father, to be fair) trotted out this list—earthquakes, nuclear fallout, plastic surgery . . . Let's just say I was young, impressionable, and to be honest, not completely positive film was my bag. I mean, I'd tried getting my feet wet with the video thing, and that wasn't the greatest success story you ever heard. The kicker was, there would be no support, "monetarily or otherwise," if I decided to move out to L.A. to try my hand at the silver screen. Without the coin, or the inclination to figure out how to raise some, a sojourn out there became sort of moot. I don't know why I wasn't more proactive about the whole thing. I could have been Sofia Coppola by now probably. Best not to think about it.

The ski patrollers in their red jackets with the big white plus signs on the back were mingling among us. I caught Bob, with his big, bushy, blond handlebar mustache, checking me out. "Betty," he called. "I'll be over on Après Vous later if you want to take a couple of runs."

That wasn't the kind of thing he usually said when Jack was around. Bob and I had this clandy thing going where we'd grab the occasional run together. Sometimes he'd take me down trails early, before anyone else had skied them, to help put up ropes and mark rocks with bamboo poles. Every once in a while, he'd drop by the Moose when I was working and buy me a shot of Jaeger. The last time he'd come in, he'd sat next to my station at the bar sipping Bass and doing shots for like two hours. Finally, when he was good and drunk, he looked at me blearily and said, "Betty, I wanna talk to ya about something."

I kept putting him off, checking and rechecking my tables to give the impression I was extra busy. Because that was *one* conversation I did *not* want to have. The unspoken thing was cool. I *liked* that Bob had a crush on me, enjoyed his company and all that. He was a sweet guy. And a ski patroller, which made him mountain royalty. He was married, though, with two kids. And he wasn't separated. Not that *that* was what was holding me back. I don't think I would have been interested in starting anything with him even if he *wasn't* married.

I don't know when I became a magnet for married men, I swear. Back in New York, I didn't even *know* any married men. I'd never even *been* with a guy older than myself now that I think of it, much less married and, in Bob's case, with kids. I imagine that sort of thing happens more frequently in ski towns. The reason I think that is because people can get pretty bored in these resort communities. I'm not talking about the ones who are happily married, have their lives all figured out, and know what they're doing there (although I've seen some of them lose it too). It's the ones like me, in the "developmental stage" as it were, who can wind up waist deep in their own excrement. And it has nothing to do with age. I knew a lot of people over forty who were *still* trying to figure out what to do with their lives. Whereas in New York, everyone's on the way *somewhere*, and there's barely a second to think about any damn thing, everyone's so keyed up all the time.

I felt this tingly surge of guilt. Not because anything had ever happened between Bob and me. Okay, let me amend that.

Over the summer, before Jack, Bob had taken me for a drive one night in his beautiful old Cadillac convertible after my shift at the Moose was over. "I want to show you something," he'd said.

Now usually, when a guy wants to take you for a ride in his convertible to "show you something," he's got something up his sleeve. But Bob was a pretty simple guy. I knew he wasn't going to attack me or anything. We drove in silence, sipping our Myers's and OJs from Go-Cups. Up and up the pass between Wilson, Wyoming, and Victor, Idaho, we went, switching back and forth for what seemed like a really long time. We'd been driving for about twenty minutes, and I lived on the other side of the valley. He'd have to take me back to the Moose to pick up my car. I didn't want to offend him or anything, so I didn't ask any questions. Instead I stared up at the stars to keep from thinking about how late it was getting.

Finally he pulled over at a turnout, killed the engine, hopped out, opened my door, and said, "We're here." Heading toward the woods, he asked, "Hear that?"

I heard the sound of trickling water. Kneeling by a small pool next to a rock, Bob cupped his hands in the water and took a sip. "You've gotta try this," he said, scooping more water and holding it to my mouth.

"Is it okay?" I asked. I'd learned to be wary of drinking non-filtered water by that time, having experienced the shitstorm that is giardia—an intestinal infection caused, in my particular case, by drinking contaminated water.

"It's better than okay," he said. "It's heaven on earth. The best water you'll ever taste in your life."

I wasn't too smooth, slurping it out of his hands like a cow at a trough. We both started laughing. "Is that it?" I asked, my shirt wet down the front, chilling in the night air.

"That's it," he said. "I've never shown that to anyone before."

I knew, for him, it was a profound moment. It was sort of profound for me too, drinking from a secret spring out there in the crisp summer Wyoming night. But there was also something about the simplicity of what it took to please him. It sort of made me sad. Not that I'm some great complex character. I don't know, it's hard to explain. Maybe I'm just harder to please.

Back in the car, Bob leaned across the wide expanse of the front seat and gave me a soft kiss on the cheek. That was as close as we'd ever come.

Jack wasn't paying attention anyway. He was discussing the new Völkl G4 powder parabolics with Speed. He didn't even really know Bob.

We all watched as the big, red, square tram, JACKSON HOLE in bold white lettering, approached the bay. The boys in red jokingly called, "Make way for the ski patrol."

It was true they took precedence over any of us. It was a good thing most of them were good guys. Oh, and Smitty, but she was guylike. Getting on the Jackson Hole ski patrol was no easy matter for anyone, but I imagined it must have been that much harder for her. Like being the first girl to work on a submarine, or join a fraternity or something.

The stairs up to the tram bay were corrugated metal, fairly treacherous in clunky plastic boots. People took baby steps, carrying their poles in one hand, their skis clamped together by safety breaks in the other. The doors opened, and the throng made its way forward, a smattering of low and high "moos" and "baaaaas."

The doors closed and the tram thrust itself forward and high into the sky, swinging back and forth gently as the box steadied itself to the upward momentum. People chatted quietly about the weather, and the sick partying they'd done the night before, while over the speakers the Grateful Dead sang, "Shake it, shake it, Sugaree, just don't tell 'em you know me . . ."

The tram conductor began, "Good morning, ladies and gentlemen. You are aboard the Jackson Hole tram. The temperature at the top this morning is minus fifteen degrees Fahrenheit, wind speed, twenty-five miles per hour. The visibility is moderate. There are six to twelve fresh inches of powder at the top. Conditions are windswept and variable, with powder predominating."

Whoops and hollers.

"Ladies and gentlemen, all runs from the top of the Jackson Hole tram are expert and above. If you are on this tram by mistake, another tram will be along in approximately ten minutes to take you back down to the bottom. Follow the green dots for the easiest route down. All runs from the top are *open*."

"That's what I'm talkin' about," Speed said.

As we pulled into the bay at the top, small snow tornadoes whipped around the tram. The scene out the window was otherworldly—the vegetation not covered by snow stunted and craggy. The doors slid open, and the cargo, too excited to mince their way slowly over the slippery corrugated metal, moved out quick. A couple of people slipped, no one fell. As the cold wind ripped at our faces, we lowered our goggles and pulled up our neck gaiters. When freshies were to be had, there was no time to waste.

Banging the snow off the bottoms of our boots, we clamped into bindings and strapped into boards. "You in?" Jack asked.

"Yup," I said.

When Speed was attached to his uniski, Jack held out his pole to help get him started. "Much obliged, brother!" Speed called back as he tore ass into the mist.

The secret to skiing powder is "point 'em." That is, instead of turning right away, you want to keep your tips in the fall line. Otherwise, the heaviness of the snow will slow you down, preventing you from working into the up, down rhythm that skiing mounds of new snow requires. It's the first thing I learned, and to this day, whenever I'm standing at the top of a virgin expanse, "point 'em" is the last thing I think before diving in.

Now I love powder. Can hardly enjoy skiing without it. I am a powder snob, powder pig, powder hound. My friends back east don't get it. They're content to tough it out through a gauntlet of howling snowmaking machines, on trails groomed within an inch of their lives. I just can't do it anymore. I've been ruined.

Jack and Speed had already disappeared. Jack could ski better and faster than just about anyone I knew. Except maybe Speed. He was always just this side of control, on the verge of killing himself, pulling these brilliant last-second maneuvers to keep from wiping.

Skiing the traverse along the top of Rendezvous Bowl, I

scoped out the terrain below, trying to determine the best line. The sound of chattering skis scraping along the windblown traverse was almost drowned out by the low hum of velocity. Moving across that way was a study in anticipation, like waiting for the ketchup to come.

Without losing momentum I dove into the thick, light powder, staying on top of the skis as they floated and sunk, floated and sunk... my line was open, the surface of the snow smooth. It was face shot city. (In mountain, as opposed to porn, terms, a face shot is what happens when there's so much powder it flies up and hits you in the face, occasionally impeding your ability to inhale.) A snorkel would have been just the thing, and although I'd heard about some crazy powder hounds using them back in the old days, I couldn't say I'd ever seen anybody wearing one.

Jack and Speed were waiting at the roped off entrance to the Hobacks, Speed's sketchy facial hair already caked and icing with snow. "How 'bout it?" he asked, his face euphoric.

"Sucks," I said.

"Big time," Jack said, ducking under the rope. They kept it cordoned off at all times, whether the Hobacks were open or not.

The rocks were well covered, the boughs of the pine trees heavy underneath ledges of snow. This time we kept the traverse short. There was no need to go searching for fresh tracks this morning, and the farther out we went, the more of a hump we'd have at the bottom.

"The Hobacks" refers to three vast, ungroomed ridges on the southern part of the mountain that has more of an "out of bounds" feel. The ski patrol monitors the area closely, and closes it down when the conditions get dicey. For Jackson locals, the Hobacks are what it's all about.

That morning, the clouds still hadn't lifted, so it was like skiing through milky pea soup. The coverage was good enough that we didn't have to worry about the poor visibility. The chances of hitting a rock or tree out there were slim. Trusting your skis to guide you safely under those conditions is the definition of blind faith.

Jack, Speed, and I took turns leading and breaking, watching one another from above and below. I'm not sure if any of us would have admitted it, but it was a real catwalk. As anyone who's halfway decent can attest, the only thing sweeter than busting through piles of snow like a rock star is having an audience while you're doing it.

chapter 7

We were lined up in our powder blue instructors' uniforms with name tags on our chests by 9:30 A.M. Hoss Barlow, a rancher in the off-season, and Margaret MacDonald, a.k.a. Mac, one of the strongest cyclists in the valley, stood in front of us brandishing clipboards. The two of them effectively ran the program under the direction of the legendary Pepi Stiegler, the Austrian gold medalist, who could be seen out and around flashing his pearly whites.

The only time I, personally, had anything to do with Pepi was during the pre-season clinic, when our technique was evaluated on video—the dashing Pepi pointing out an inconsistent pole plant here, a lack of proper steering there. All of us first-years, who secretly imagined ourselves second only to Bode Miller, were quickly disabused of our hotdogging notions. I suppose a little humility isn't a bad thing when it comes to ski-

ing. You can't take it too far though. Without certain knowledge that you are capable of kicking serious ass, things would
start to deteriorate pretty quickly.

I guess now wouldn't be a bad time to discuss what I like
to call the skier ethos. That is, no one wants to look like a
meathead on the boards. Hot skiers might be total duds
as human beings, but putting their moves down on the hill,
they are, for better or worse, superstars. The opposite is
also true. You could be the most magnificent person in the
world, but if you're flailing, mountain cred will allude you. It's
not pretty. It's not fair. But there you have it—survival of the
fittest.

The primary allure to being a ski instructor was the season
pass—a value of something like sixteen hundred bucks. It was
this perk that attracted primarily recent college grads, with a
smattering of older folk dissatisfied with lives in the "real
world," to try out at the preseason clinic. They sure weren't
doing it for the money. First-years made $6.50 an hour for
groups and $12.50 an hour for privates. Which never made
much sense to me. Why wouldn't you make more teaching a
group when you had more people paying for a lesson? Anyway.
We could ski all day every day, but we'd have to do time teaching kids and beginners. None of us were certified, so the highest level we could teach was intermediate. Watching Jack lead
a group of three-year-olds down the mountain was pretty cute,
(a) because he was good with kids, and (b) because he was
such an amazing skier that he could make even snowplowing
look cool.

On any given morning, Hoss was the guy you wanted to be

with, because he handled the grown-ups. Mac was in charge of the kids' program. Some instructors preferred teaching kids. But give me a cardiologist from Philly over a spoiled six-year-old from Manhattan any old day of the week. I enjoyed the psychoanalysis that went along with teaching grown-ups better. You could get to the bottom of a few pretty disturbing neuroses in two hours.

Hoss said, "Winters, you head over with Mac to SKIwee. Jack Catcher, you stay over here with me."

I could see Barb over in the pen, her butt bulging out of a pair of navy blue stretchies, quieting down a bunch of five-year-olds. She was older than most of us, had abandoned Park Avenue and a guy she didn't want to marry. I thought she was kind of a wiseacre until I realized how insecure she was. She wasn't the best skier in the group, but skiing ability didn't matter as much as being able to communicate with your pupils, which it turned out, she did quite well.

I'm pretty insecure myself if you want to know. People might think I'm outgoing and hard-core, but the truth is, I second-guess myself all the time. I think it's almost a *sign* of insecurity to come off looking all tough, like nothing can touch you, the way I do sometimes.

Trudging behind Mac to the SKIwee corral, I saw Hoss pairing Jack off in a private with a slim beauty. A little snow bunny decked in what looked like a Bogner ensemble—fuchsia stretchies, a matching fitted pink jacket, and a powder blue headband showcasing her Farrah Fawcett-Majors. Jack shrugged at me and waved. The woman had a look of rapture on her face as though, from all of the hunky instructors lined up that morning to give privates, Jack was the one she'd been praying for.

I couldn't say I blamed her. I could see women paying to spend time with Jack, I really could. I mean he was no Chippendale, but that's not the kind of guy most women go for anyway (not me at least). He had the lean muscle tone of a cyclist, more like one of those Calvin Klein or Ralph Lauren models. I could have been jealous, but he'd never given me any reason to be. I was more relieved that he was pulling in a private. You could generally count on a tip with a private. Especially if your student had the hots for you.

We'd spent a chunk of the month's savings to register Jack's truck. I was already working six days a week instructing, and three nights cocktailing at the Moose. It was the first time in my life that I had to worry about money. And let me tell you, it was wearing me out. I'd become totally obsessed with not having it, wondering how and where I was going to get it, and whether we'd have enough of it to pay for car insurance and groceries.

It wasn't where I'd come from. I mean my dad was a partner in a corporate law firm and a pretty wealthy guy. I hadn't been spoiled or anything. Well, not too spoiled anyway. One thing was certain—I'd never had to worry about buying groceries before. Jack and I tried to do most of our eating and drinking at the Moose, where we ate and drank for free.

Mac turned and said, "Hey, I've been meaning to talk to you about something."

"Uh-oh," I said.

"Don't worry. It's nothing bad."

"Phew."

"I wanted to know if you were planning on trying out for the Pete Laurey shoot."

Pete Laurey was a Warren Miller protégé who made extreme ski videos. I'd seen the Xerox posted in the lockers—"If you've got a pair, we want to see 'em! Extreme rippers wanted to debut . . ." Despite the sexist language, women were encouraged to apply. And it was about time too. You hardly ever saw women in those videos. It really got my goat.

The thing was, competition made me nervous. I could still remember having to drop out of the swim team when I was ten because I hurled before every meet. Same with horse shows. I was drawn to individual sports, but I couldn't really take the pressure. It was almost like the more people expected of me, the less I was capable of achieving. The opposite was also true. In sports like field hockey, where the responsibility for winning is spread across an entire team, I turned into a real powerhouse. It's got to be psychological. "I hadn't planned on it."

"Well, Pete's a friend of mine. He's asked me to recommend people. I want to recommend you."

I looked down at her, she was about five foot two. I think I'm a pretty decent skier. Not the best there is, but not bad. And not just for a girl. I was flattered and thought a little fishing trip might be in order. "You think I'm good enough?"

"I wouldn't have askedya if I didn't think you were good enough," she said, casually jabbing me with her gloved forefinger.

"I don't know. It's not really my scene."

"Oh. Getting paid to travel the globe, skiing the gnarliest peaks with some of the hottest skiers in the world isn't your *scene*, huh. I see. I get it."

"It's not that—"

What it was . . . I could handle steep, I could handle narrow, I could handle bumps and adverse conditions. I just wasn't too stoked about catching big air. Those guys you see jumping off hundred-foot cliffs and whatnot? Not my bag.

"I don't want to hear any excuses! As your boss, I *order* you to at *least* try out. What do you have to lose?"

"I could die," I joked. Not very funny, actually. Given the context.

"Yeah, 'cause if you don't try out, I'm gonna *kill* you. You've got some time. Just tell me you'll think about it."

"What about Jack?"

"Doesn't he bike race in the summer?"

"Yeah."

"I don't think he can do both, but it can't hurt for him to try out."

"Will you recommend him?"

"I'll put in a word."

"Then I'll think about it."

"Good deal."

I could hear the shrieking before I saw the little girl wearing an expensive snow white one-piece with a fluffy white bunny hat, the ears sticking up lopsided from her head. She was in hysterics, her father on both knees in the snow trying to calm her. Mac was down on the ground there too. I think kids related to her because she sort of looked like one of them. Turning to me, she asked, "Do you mind?"

"Not at all," I said, even though I knew I'd probably wind up dumping the little brat in Kinderschule to get wired on hot chocolate and animal crackers before the lesson even began. It was where we took kids who couldn't be cajoled into skiing. Mostly four-, five-, and six-year-olds who didn't like skiing in the first place and felt abandoned by their parents. Which most of them were.

"Looks like you gotta live one." It was Lynne, one of my best buddies and the only other girl instructor I skied with because we were about the same level, slogging by with her own group of kids.

The little Shirley Temple throwing the tantrum looked to be about four. Her back was down in the snow as she flailed her arms and legs, kicking at her father's knee at intervals with her tiny boot. I was in no mood.

"This is Candy," Mac said, holding out both hands as if to say, "Ta da!"

"Candy," she said, raising her voice, "this is Betty! She's going to take you skiing!"

"Hi, Candy," I said, kneeling next to her father, who gave me a grief-stricken look.

Brother. Barb was the woman for this situation. I was fairly certain I'd only make the kid feel worse.

"Candy honey, say hi to Betty," her father said, trying for distraction.

"No! No! No! No Netty!" she screamed in her own dialect. "Ni no nont Netty!"

"Candy sweetie, that's not very nice," her father said, catching her boot as it was about to come down, once again, on his knee.

"Maybe you should go," I whispered. "It'll be fine." I had to lie like that to parents all the time. I mean sometimes it *was* fine. But in cases like Candy's I could pretty well predict it would *not* be. The minute her father was out of sight, it was Kinderschule here we come.

As he moved away though, Candy's screams abated. Barb came up and said, "I can take her with my group if you want."

"It's okay. I can handle it." I didn't want Barb making me look bad.

"It's your call."

"Thanks, Barbarella. I'm all over it." Laying down next to her in the snow, I asked, "How old are you, Candy?" That was the first thing we always asked.

Pressing her lips together, she stared straight ahead and didn't answer.

"Are you *two*?" I asked, holding up two gloved fingers.

She shook her head.

I knew that would get her. Kids her age never want you to think they're younger. "Are you *one*?"

"No! Four!" she said, holding up four little fingers.

"Wow! Four years old! You're really big!" At least she'd stopped crying. "Whataya say we ride up in the chair together?"

She was sniffling, her breath catching in little hiccups, and when she sat up to look at me, I could see a booger the size of a large slug moving in and out of her nose. "Here." Taking off my glove and pulling a Kleenex out of my pocket, I held it up to her nose and said, "Blow."

She blew.

"There, that's better," I said, folding up the slug and sticking it into my pocket.

"You look funny," she said.

"Do I?" I asked, sitting up, pulling my Patagonia rooster hat over to one side.

"What's your name again?"

"Betty. You can call me Betty Cheddy. That'll help you remember it."

Screwing up her face, she said, "Betty Cheddy?"

"Like the cheese," I said. "You know cheddar cheese?"

She nodded and sniffled a few more times.

"Why don't we put your mittens on, okay?" Her hands were wet and red from digging into the snow. The mittens were attached across the inside back of her jacket with a piece of string. She let me put them on and sheepishly followed me toward the rest of my group—a couple of motley three-year-olds wearing helmets and miniature skis. "Who needs an Edgie Wedgie?" (Edgie Wedgies are cylindrical pieces of rubber about six inches long that screw onto the tips of skis, holding them close together to make snowplowing easier.)

"I do!" they both shouted.

Candy looked up at me and asked, "Do I need an Eggy Weggy?"

"We'll see. I'll bring an extra one with me just in case." Candy was a little big for the device. It was mostly for really small kids who didn't have enough muscle control yet. But I'd let her use one if it would make her feel better.

Shuffling toward the chairlift, I got a couple of people who looked like they knew what they were doing to ride up with the three-year-olds. That's when Candy started to cry. "Ni nowanna go on da *naaaair*."

I now saw that it was probably the idea of taking the chair that had Candy frightened to begin with. I couldn't say I blamed her. They could be pretty scary. I'm amazed that more people don't injure themselves on those things. They're like big metal monsters that whip around, scoop you up, and spit you out at the top. One false move and whack! A karate chop to the back of the calf. And that's not the worst of it. If you spaz and miss your mark, you can be dragged, flung, Frisbeed, clocked in the head.

Say you conquer your fear and by the grace of God actually manage to *board* the chair. Then it's up, up, and away! Where you spend the rest of the ride envisioning your disastrous debarkation at dizzying heights while clinging to a freezing iron bar. If you have vertigo, you're shit out of luck. Any way you slice it, there's a good chance that, if you're a beginner, you're putting yourself in danger of suffering some lumps and bumps. Humiliation is par for the course.

Kids are different though. They're more malleable, and they have a shorter distance to fall. And when they do fall, they get over it. They don't brood and overthink things the way grownups do. "It's okay, Candy, don't be scared. I'm right here. I'll help you get on." I felt sort of ridiculous calling her Candy. Who names a kid that?

"You *hold* me."

"I'll hold on to you tight. Don't worry. You'll do great."

This was what the job was all about. Positive reinforcement. With kids and adults. Except with big people you had to throw in a few more technicalities—head up, weight on the downhill ski, knees bent, hips pointing down the mountain, angulate! Steer! Carve! Phantom Move! Little Toe Edge! Grown-ups really cling to stuff like that. It helps get them over their biggest hurdle—*Fear*. In the instructors' clinics, they even break it down into Fear One and Fear Two. Fear One being the physiological response to fear, the adrenaline, the palpitating heartbeat, cold sweats, and so on. As opposed to Fear Two, which is the psychological brain blitz that occurs when you're looking down a steep, narrow chute for instance, saying to yourself, "No fucking *way*."

Most adult beginners aren't getting anywhere close to a steep, narrow chute, yet their fear response can be the same, even if the hill is practically flat. It's all about your threshold.

For me, personally, the only way to conquer fear is to have an attack-the-hill response. That is, if I'm standing on top of some scary looking pitch, I try not to dillydally there too long thinking about it. A big fear squelcher is to get on in there and start making turns. It's a pretty good life lesson, I think. Take action, right? It always makes you feel more together and in control. In that sense, skiing really is a metaphor for life.

Candy was scared, but I could see with a little special attention she'd get with the program. We were next on line for the chair, so I gently placed my hand on her shoulder and guided her out. I nodded to the lifty, and he brought the speed down so that the chair was practically at a standstill when it came to us. Scooping Candy up, I pushed her snugly back, and away we went.

"I did it!" Candy said, looking at me with the most beautiful smile.

I thought she might be warming up to me. Which naturally made me want to give her the best lesson of her four-year-old life. "Of course you did! See? I knew you could!"

By the end of the lesson, Candy was laughing and leading the troops down the bunny hill.

Later, while I was giving another lesson, I heard someone calling, "Neddy na Neddy!"

Looking up, I saw Candy and her dad waving from the chair. "Thank you very much!" the dad called.

"You're welcome!" I called back. It felt good to be appreciated every once in a while.

In the lockers, Dan, the joker from Jersey, was glumly swallowing forkfuls of Hormel chili straight from the can as part of what he liked to call his "cowboy mystique."

"Who-*wee*! The girl's got an appetite," he said, watching me scarf down the chicken and pickle sandwich. Sunny and Bo carried in the handicap ski sled. They taught special needs skiers and were, in my opinion, the biggest heroes on the mountain next to ski patrollers.

Jack stuck his head in to let me know his morning private had turned into an all day.

No surprise there.

Lynne clunked up, raising her goggles. "Hey, Betty, wanna catch a tram?"

"What am I, David Lee Roth?" Dan asked, grabbing her around the waist. Like a few of the other guys, he had a crush on her. Couldn't say I blamed him. She was tall, lean, and strong, with high cheekbones, clear blue eyes, and long strawberry blond hair worn mostly in a single braid down the middle of her back. She also happened to be loaded. Family money from way back when. Too bad she didn't like guys.

"I wasn't talking to you, stinker," she said, pinching his nose.

"Whataya say, shredder? Expert chutes are supposed to be sa-*hweet*."

"Let's do it," I said.

"I guess you can come too if you want," she said to Dan.

"No. Forget it. You missed your chance to hang with the large *salam*, ladies," Dan said, grabbing his package.

"Large like *this*?" Lynne said, holding up her pinkie.

"Oh, girl . . . you don't know what I'd do to you."

"I'm sure you'd make me scream. And not in a good way."

"What is this, douche on Dan day?"

"Are you coming or what?" I asked. We only had an hour before afternoon lessons started.

"If you two think I'm going to drop everything just to ski with you," he said, giving us an incredulous look, "you're absofuckinglutely right!"

Standing at the top of the Expert Chutes, Dan said, "Ladies? *Observe*," and jumped in. There was no denying the guy could ski. He fit right into my short, powerful legs theory. Which is that people with short, powerful legs have an advantage over the rest of us. Something to do with their center of gravity.

"Damn," Lynne said. "Look at *him*. We can't let that stand." Using her poles, she hopped over the lip and boogied down into the trees. Her legs were longer than Dan's, but she skied just as well. Which brings me to another theory. That people who learn to ski in the East tend to be shredders, because they've had the worst of it. In a way, though, it's kind of apples and oranges, because the snow conditions out west require a whole different learning curve.

It was my turn. I surveyed the bump layout, registering the positions of the trees. I'd been thinking about Pete Laurey all morning, but I still wasn't convinced I had what it took. And even if I did, I wasn't sure I wanted to take it any further.

Launching myself into the chute, I took the bumps head-on slowing myself down for the tree and the blind spot. You never knew who might be stalled where you least expected it. Hitting another skier was just about the worst thing you could do. Except maybe smacking into a tree. And then, only if you Bonoed.

Lynne and Dan were already down below, waiting and watching. The rest of the trail was open. Letting my skis go, I lifted them up into my chest, catching minor air over a rock and landing well, theatrically spraying Lynne and Dan before coming to a stop.

Dan shook his head. "Hoochie *mama*," he said.

"What," Lynne said. "Now we're *both* hoochie mamas? Make up your mind whydontcha?"

"Ladies, ladies, please," he said, grabbing his package once again, "there's enough of the horse to go around."

"Dream on, Dan," I said, purposefully skiing over his tails, on down to the quad, where we slipped into the ski school line.

Labarge, the lifty, held up his hand to the next four people in line. "Hold up a minute," he said, motioning to us with his chin to come ahead. "You guys doin' a clinic?" he asked, smiling.

We weren't supposed to have lift privileges unless we were giving a lesson, but none of the lifties enforced that rule.

"That's right," Dan said. "The 'how high you can get' clinic."

"Right on, spunky," Labarge said, holding the chair back so it slid perfectly under our butts.

"That guy gives good chair," I said. I really appreciated the lifties that took the job seriously.

Halfway to the top, Dan lit up a spliff and handed it to Lynne. Taking a toke, she held it out to me and asked, "You trying out for Pete Laurey?"

"I don't know."

"I was thinking about it," she said.

"You should," I said, handing the joint back to Dan.

"I'll do it if you'll do it," she said.

"Why is this even a *question*?" Dan asked, using the joint for emphasis.

"Are *you* doing it?" Lynne asked.

"Do you have to ask?" he said, sucking in his cheeks and giving us his best Clark Gable.

"Figures," Lynne said. "Why are guys so cocky? You probably didn't even think twice about trying out, did you?"

"Getting paid to travel around the world and ski? Hmm, let me *think* about that," he said, stroking an imaginary beard with his hand. "Not!"

chapter 8

By 2:00 P.M. I was ready to hit the sack. Luckily I still had forty-five minutes to catch some shut-eye before my shift at the Moose started. After moving the truck from the employee lot to the one next to the kitchen entrance, I killed the engine. The sun had already disappeared behind the mountains, making the light a sort of dim gray-orange. I imagine if you were feeling a bit more chipper than I was, it would be a pretty nice time of day. Like if you were gearing up to *drink* a few margs, rather than *serve* them.

Jack kept a mattress, sleeping bags, and pillows in the back at all times. You never knew when you might need to crash. It was too cold back there though. Grabbing a pillow and sleeping bag, I curled up on the bench seat in front and tried to sleep.

I don't know. I'm not so sure the Beatles were right when

they sang, "All you need is love." Because you can have love and still not feel so hot. Let's face it, that whole "free spirit" excuse worked a lot better when I was drinking or getting stoned. Not so well when I was curled up in the front seat of the truck at the end of the day, waiting for my next shift to begin. Those naps I took in the Moose parking lot before my shift were some pretty depressing times. The afternoon light I'll never forget. It felt like dying. It wasn't the work I minded so much, more the fact that even with all that work, we were barely getting by. I mean, how can you slave your ass off all day and all night, and still not be able to afford health care? That crushed me.

I wondered what I could do to remedy the situation. Maybe I needed to go back to school and get some kind of graduate degree or something. That would start a whole other anxiety fest concerning what I'd go to graduate school for.

I'd been dreaming about guzzling ice-cold water from fountains and pitchers of lemonade when I woke up freezing with fifteen minutes to spare. After changing into a miniskirt, one of those spandex bodysuits that crawl up your butt, a pair of black stockings, and leather flats, I slip-slided my way to the kitchen door.

The Moose is an enormous structure—the bar-restaurant upstairs, various shops and the Rocky Mountain Oyster downstairs. The bar itself was two stories high, decorated with license plates from all over the country, old metal gas station signs, and a stuffed moose hitched up to a sleigh hanging from the ceiling. A zydeco band would be playing later that night. It was three o'clock, après-ski was just about to start, Robert Palmer singing, "Hey, hey, Julia, you're actin' so peculia . . ."

The whole cocktail thing had taken me a while to get used to. Basically, I'm not going to lie, I was one of the worst waitresses I'd ever seen, cocktail or otherwise. I really admire good waiting skills. You've got to be organized, on top of it. And I guess, by that point, I wasn't so bad. But you should have seen me when I first started. The head bartender, Daisy Duke, hassled me until I got my act together. Old Daisy really couldn't stand me at first, I could tell. She was one of those pretty southern girls who'd been tending bar all her life practically, and had no patience for the likes of my East Coast, college-educated ass.

The thing was, cocktailing at the Moose was as close to brain surgery as I was likely to come. I kid you not. There was this whole system of ordering drinks that Daisy referred to as the Vegas Method—calling the drinks in order of the types of glasses they came in. That way, the bartender could pull them with maximum efficiency. I had to make up a word— HIROFATA: high, rocks, fat, tall—to remember it all. Then you called beer, then wine, then coffee drinks and cordials.

As if that wasn't enough of a brainteaser, you'd then have to work out the totals broken down into three categories—liquor, beer and wine, coffee and cordials—at top speed, and repeat them to the bartender in a loud, clear voice. If you were up there waiting, you damn well better be ready to give your order, or dirty looks *would* be thrown. Those bartenders were a bunch of ballbusters.

We weren't allowed to wear pants, and the shorter the skirt, the better the tips. Some girls got pretty slutty with their outfits. Leslie swore by fishnets and high-heeled cowboy boots.

She had this whole routine where she'd pretend to drop her pen or a napkin or something and flash guys her G-string when she bent down to pick it up. That girl made a lot of dough.

Me? I didn't even know what a G-string was until Daisy gave me one of her old ones. You could count on Daisy for stuff like that. Over the summer I'd gone out and splurged on this spandex cotton dress that fit me like the proverbial skin on a grape. It made underwear look like diapers. So Daisy pulled me aside and told me it was either the G-string or nothing. Panty lines weren't good for business. It took a while to get used to the idea of having a piece of fabric wedged up my ass. But what Daisy said was true. "Once it's up there, you don't feel a thing."

I did okay with the tips. Not great. I might clear a hundred and fifty bucks on a good night. But then you had to tip out the bartender, and I always went overboard with that, because the last thing I wanted any of them to think was that I was cheap.

Daisy and I had the upstairs bar that night. It'd taken us a while, but we liked working with each other by that time. I'd become fairly proficient with the system, and I think Daisy credited herself with training me. She deserved the credit too.

"Betty Boop! You look like somethin' the cat dragged in."

"I appreciate that, Daisy Duke." Her real name was Una Gordon, but everyone called her Daisy Duke. I'm not sure how it all started, but everyone on staff pretty much went by a double name—Billy Bob, Bobby Joe, Peggy Sue—it really was like *The Dukes of Hazzard* in that place.

"Somethin' a shot of tequila might cure?" She was arranging bottles of beer in the ice sink behind the bar.

"Might." Daisy was good about doling out the free shots.

Bringing her face up close, she said, "I'm serious, sweetheart, you really don't look too good."

Now that she mentioned it, I guess I'd felt better. "I'm beat," I said.

"How about a tea with lemon or somethin'?"

"That sounds good."

Daisy was allowed to wear whatever she wanted, usually opting for a pair of skintight Wranglers and a belly shirt. She had one of those compact, cute little figures.

I took a few sips of tea and began wiping down my tables, dispersing candles from a tray. They were the lantern kind, made of that rough red glass you had to stick your fingers inside of to light.

I put one on each table, then went around with a pack of matches burning my fingers. I arranged a pile of cocktail napkins and swizzle sticks on the side of my station, checked the lemons, limes, twists, cherries, onions, and olives in the tray. I needed a twenty for my bank.

"Daisy honey, sweetie?"

She gave me a long stare and said, "I do not think I'm gonna like what's comin'."

"Front me a twenty?"

"You're lucky I'm in a good mood," she said, popping open the register. We cocktail waitresses had to start off with our own twenties. That way, it was impossible to cheat the bar. You could cheat *customers*, but it took me a while to figure that out. Sometimes, if a table wasn't tipping, I'd tack on an extra dollar a round. Leslie taught me about that. I didn't have to do it very often, though. The après-ski crowd tended to be good tippers.

"You're lookin' pale. Go down to the kitchen and have Marty fix you a steak. You need some blood," Daisy said.

"I'm not hungry."

Picking up the bar phone she said, "I'm telling Marty you're on your way down to give him your order. I want you on top of it tonight."

I'd really gotten to like Daisy. She had a major flirtation going with Billy Bob, the bar manager. Those two liked to carry on in public as though something was going on between them, yet both had significant others who didn't seem to mind. Daisy and I bonded over horses. I rode English, and she was a Western-riding barrel racer, which she promised to teach me one day.

Heading back into the kitchen, I could hear Marty talking to Alice and Pam, the preppy prep girls. "Ladies, ladies," he said, taking the knife from Pam, "you don't wanna chop that parsley too fine or it winds up tasting like mowed grass," he said, demonstrating. "Like that. See?"

They nodded in silence.

"Can I hear 'yes, Chef'?"

"Yes, Chef," they said, in bored unison.

"What's up, little lady?" he asked, his fingers going through the parsley. "You look like you just saw a ghost."

The kitchen smelled like charbroiled beef and fried onions. I couldn't say it was whetting my appetite. "You think I could have a steak tonight?"

"Honey, you know you can have a steak any night you want."

I did know that, I just didn't like to take advantage.

"How you want it cooked? The usual? Medium rare?"

"That'd be good."

"Baked potato? We got grilled zucchini as a side tonight."

"Great," I said, but just hearing him talk about food made me want to hork.

"Have that ready forya in about ten minutes."

"I'll be back in ten." The rest of the crew was eating the staff meal in the restaurant, which usually consisted of some sort of pasta and all you wanted to eat from the salad bar.

My legs felt like lead. I didn't know how I was going to make it through the night.

When my steak was ready, I took it upstairs and sat at one of the small, round tables overlooking the downstairs bar. I'd brought along a bottle of A1, hoping to make it more appetizing. As I moved the knife back and forth through the thick slab, I spotted Jack and Farrah, sitting near the fire having a gay old time.

Dragging the morsel through a small pool of A1, I popped it in my mouth and started to chew . . . Pushing back from the table, I took the plate up to the bar, dumped the whole thing into the garbage, and went downstairs to introduce myself.

Farrah looked like she'd just gotten off a tanning bed, her eyes pulled up into a fixed look of surprise.

Jack saw me coming. "Betty!" he called, waving. "Hey, I want you to meet Charlene, or should I call you Suzy Chapstick?"

He sounded like he'd had a few. The two of them giggled. I couldn't say I'd ever seen Jack giggle before. He wasn't a giggler.

"I'm Betty," I said, sticking out my hand, trying to be friendly even though I felt like barfing for more reasons than one.

"*Betty.*" Charlene was laughing so hard she could barely

catch her breath. "I just *love* that name," she said, dabbing tears from the corners of her eyes.

"Did I miss something?" I asked.

"I swear, I don't think I've had anyone improve so much in one day," Jack said, giving her the winning Catcher smile.

"Oh, go on," Charlene said, waving him away.

"I'm serious, I wouldn't just say that," he said.

"He wouldn't," I confirmed. A full-day private was about as much money as you could make as a ski instructor, and Charlene had hired him on for the week. If he played his cards right, he'd be in for a big tip.

"Charlene here is a regular Picabo Street."

"I better get back," I said. We weren't allowed to sit down on the job, and I needed to take a quick load off before things got busy. "It was nice meeting you, Charlene."

"Oh, likewise I'm sure."

"Wait, B," Jack said, grabbing my hand. Standing, he whispered, "You okay?"

"What is it with everyone tonight? Do I really look that bad?"

"You don't have your usual glow," he said.

"That'll be great for tips." Peering around him, I waved at Charlene and said, "Nice meeting you. Jack, I've gotta head."

"Hold up, hold up," he said. "You know I think you're beautiful no matter what, right?"

"Right," I said smiling, backing up to go.

"Don't you forget it! I'll come up before I leave," he called. "Speed's giving me a ride home."

"Not if I can help it," Charlene growled.

I don't remember giving her a look, but I must have because

as I walked away she said, "Just kidding, Betty! Nice meeting you too!"

Bob showed up at my station with a couple of the other boys from ski patrol. They were drinking the usual—pitchers of Coors with shots of Crown Royal. It was funny how many of those guys had big, bushy mustaches. If a guy on the mountain had one of those telltale stashes, odds were, he was a troller.

"Helsin, man, the guy had it coming," Jorgy said. He was a big, brawny redhead and one of the older guys on the squad. "That guy's cheated death more times . . . not a day goes by I don't hear about that knucklehead setting off an avalanche somewhere. Never hear about it neither till someone else reports it. Far be it from him to keep us informed. Pretty chatty when he needed to be hauled outa somewhere though, I'll tellya."

"All that new snow on top of two weeks of high pressure? You go out there on a day like today and you're just *askin'* for it," Bob said. "Backcountry reported avie danger was the highest it's been all season."

"Are we sure he's gone?" one of the younger guys asked. He didn't use the word *dead*. Even though it didn't sound like this guy Helsin had made too many friends, they all looked pretty grim about it anyway. People in the valley took death by avalanche pretty seriously. And most had a healthy respect for Mother Nature. The wilderness wasn't monitored. Whereas, at the resort, if you got up early enough, you could hear the patrollers setting off dynamite at dawn. The problem with skiing out of bounds is, you can take all the precautions in the world and *still* wind up dead.

"You're not dead until you're cold and dead," Jorgy said, throwing back a shot of Crown.

"Who'd you hear it from?" Bob asked.

"Smitty."

"Good source."

"Yup. Supposedly up above Fish Creek somewhere. They found his dog. And his truck parked at the turnout near the Blander Ranch."

Things were rocking in the upstairs bar with Wilson Pickett doing his version of "In the Midnight Hour," so I only caught snippets of their conversation as I made my rounds. It was a big shot night—Slippery Nipples, Sex on the Beach, Kamikazes, Russian Quaaludes, and straight up tequila and Jaeger. There was a table of traders from New York City in the corner, tipping me a fiver for every round. I had to keep them happy.

When I got back to my station, Bob was sitting on the closest stool. I almost asked him to scootch aside so I could lean an ass cheek on the edge to keep from keeling over. I'd had to go into the bathroom just to sit on the toilet with my head between my legs and splash cold water on my face twice already. I thought of the booger I'd wiped off Candy's nose . . . It had seemed harmless enough at the time, but kids were walking petri dishes of infection.

"Missedya over on Après Vous today," Bob said.

"Yeah," I said. "I decided to catch some shut-eye before my shift instead."

"Whatsa matter? You're not feeling well?" He looked concerned.

"How do I look?"

"Ah, Betty," he said, grinning, "you know you always look good to me."

"Now I *know* you're full of shit," Daisy Duke said as she poured out another round of Westbanks (double Myerses and OJs) on the rocks. "You better get your eyes checked."

"Now, Daisy, don't be jealous. You know you're up there in my top, oh, ten?"

"Top ten, huh. Can't do me any better than that?"

"All right. Call it top five."

"That's better, darlin'. For that, you get a shot of whatever you want."

"Make it Crown."

"Betty?"

I didn't really want a drink but reasoned it probably wouldn't make me feel any worse, and it might take my mind off whatever was ailing me. "Maybe I should have something with juice in it?"

"All right, how about a Sex on the Beach? There's *juice* in that," she said, winking over at Bob.

"There's the ticket," he said.

"Okay, sounds good."

"What sounds good?" Jack asked, coming around the bar and kissing me on the cheek.

"Where's your new girlfriend?" I asked.

"Crazy Charlene? Had to go to dinner."

"I bet she asked you along, didn't she?"

"As a matter of fact she did."

"And?"

"And I said no."

Bob had turned back over to Jorgy.

"You entertaining the ski patrol here?" Jack asked.

"That's an affirmative, Jacky boy. You better watch your little Chiquita, she's got quite a few fans," Daisy Duke said.

"Don't I know it," Jack said. "Can you get off early?"

"Maybe. I'm making good money though."

"Forget about the money, Betty, you need to get to bed," he said, bringing his green eyes in close, "with me."

"I'll ask Daisy when it slows down."

"I'm gonna tell Speed he can go. I'll hang out and wait for you."

"You don't have to wait."

"Of course I'll wait."

"Seriously, Jack. One of us should go home and get some sleep. Tomorrow's a long day."

He looked like he was thinking it over. "You sure?"

Actually, I wasn't sure. I would have liked to have had his company. Then again, it was practically impossible to have a conversation with anyone when things were busy. Plus, him being there just made me want to complain. "Sure," I said. "I'll be fine. I'll try to get home early."

chapter 9

The snow was coming down in big, wet, fluffy flakes when Daisy told me I could leave at ten. I was so beat I could have crawled into the back of the truck and fallen straight to sleep. I probably would have too if I wasn't so concerned about worrying Jack. Jim wouldn't answer the phone after 9:00 P.M. That was the rule. A chill had taken over my body and I couldn't get rid of it.

Wiping the snow off the windshield took the last bit of strength I had. Climbing onto the driver's seat, I blasted the heat, put the truck into four-wheel drive, and slowly pulled out of the lot. When that big vehicle was in four-wheel, you could feel the horses, the engine burning fuel. Pressing the gas pedal a little harder to make the beast move, I thought I might get away with putting it into two-high once I got out to the main road. In that weather it would take me about forty-five minutes to get home, and I didn't want to waste gas.

Snow and black ice covered the main road in intermittent patches, but for the most part, it was clear. At the stoplight at the end of the village road, I spun out a little making the turn into town. And again, merging onto Highway 89. The drive down to Hoback Junction was usually pretty peaceful at that time of night—I rarely passed another car. Good thing too, because I was sort of seeing double and wouldn't have minded having the whole road to myself—right and left sides. I popped in a mixed tape to keep myself awake and out came "Misguided Angel" by the Cowboy Junkies. No better tune to lose it to when you're feeling sorry for yourself.

As I came up on Game Creek Road, the snow blew heavy and slanted. Keeping my eyes trained on the outer white line, I followed the tracks that were already down. The road was fairly straight through that section, and I must have been doing around sixty when I saw the whites of their eyes—four deer, frozen in the headlights on the shoulder.

I slammed the brakes instead of pumping the pedal softly like you're supposed to do. The steering wheel froze, and the truck swiveled sideways as the first deer leapt out. The antilock brakes pulsed, the truck gaining momentum on the slick surface. Having lost control of the vehicle, I sat back and watched it all happen in slow motion—the front smacking the first deer in the haunches, the tail sliding sideways, thumping into a second. The sharp smell of adrenaline was in the air when the truck finally came to a stop.

All was quiet then as I watched the other two deer scamper down the trailer park road. Hitting the hazards, I pulled over as far as the snow would allow. In no rush to survey the havoc I'd wrought, I checked the rearview mirror to see if anyone was coming. The only lights were from the trailers across the way. I sat there for several seconds, the truck still in drive, my foot on the brake, thinking, I could just keep on going. Drive away.

Putting the truck in park, I got out and walked quickly back to where I'd lost control. Once I'd decided to stay, there was no time to lose. I could see a dark lump in the road in the distance. The other deer, it seemed, had gotten away.

The light-headedness made me feel calmer, as though someone else was going through the motions. The deer lifted its head, and laid it back down again. I dropped down beside it, the cold hardness of snow and dirt pressing into my stockinged knees, the miniskirt stretched tight around my thighs. Taking off a glove, I put my hand on its neck. "It's okay, girl," I said. I didn't know if it was a girl or boy or what. Don't males have antlers? Anyway, this one didn't have antlers. Her eyes were open, but her body remained totally still. "I'm sorry, girl." Seeing her alive and helpless like that gave me the same anguished pang I got when cupping a hand over a horse's eye to feel the lashes fluttering against my palm.

I didn't think I'd be able to pull her to the side of the road myself. Times like this made me wish I carried Jack's .357 Magnum everywhere. He kept it loaded, in its holster by the side of the bed, "Just in case." Something about having that gun so near almost fueled my paranoia. Like if I was alone in the cabin watching *Cheers* or something, I had that puppy resting right in my lap, waiting for someone to make my day. On car camping trips, I kept it tucked under my pillow, *Deliverance* playing over and over in my head. I knew what I'd do if anyone tried to make me squeal like a pig, boy.

Hoback Junction was only about five minutes down the road. I could drive down, get Jack and the gun, and we could deal with it. I didn't want her to lie there dying an agonizing death.

Nothing like an emergency to clear out the old cobwebs. Switching the Silverado into four-wheel, I hauled ass down to the cabin.

Mincing my way down the boot track, I noticed the porch light was the only light on. Which was strange. Usually Jack waited up for me. I didn't want to waste time but had decided I would take approximately ten seconds to change into a pair of Levi's and Sorels. The cabin door tended to stick, but I wasn't going to screw around with that. Not tonight. I rocked away and in, slamming the whole right side of my body against it. Toppling into the kitchen, I almost tripped over a small green army duffel. "Jack?" I called, switching on the kitchen light.

The refrigerator door had been left slightly ajar, which wasn't like Jack at all. He hated wasting energy. The main room was empty, so I looked over toward the bathroom, hoping to see light underneath the door. Nothing. Leaving my shell on, I wiggled out of the miniskirt and threw on a pair of jeans and Thorlos. He was probably having a drink with Speed. The gun was there on the table next to the bed where it always was, right beside *Atlas Shrugged*.

I stuck the gun with the holster into my jacket's inside pocket. The Sorels were just underneath the kitchen table near the door. I slipped them on, turned the knob, and forced the door open with my foot. The boot path over to Speed's cabin was riddled with poop from his golden retriever, Lupine, who started barking as I approached. On Speed's porch I could hear the Doors faintly singing "The End," and knew the two of them were probably watching *Apocalypse Now* for the fifty millionth time.

I knocked once and entered. It was then that I heard the hyena laugh. The three of them sat at the kitchen table, which was littered with an accumulation of empty Rolling Rock bottles. Gibby had a Budweiser mirror perched on his knee, from which he snarfed a thick, long white line through a clear plastic pen encasement.

"Betty!" Jack said, standing.

"Jack, we've gotta go," I said. I was breathing hard, like I'd just run a mile.

Holding up his hands, he said, "Don't be mad. We were just—"

"I hit a deer. It's up on eighty-nine near the trailer park. It's still alive."

"Well, whyn't you say so?" Speed said, jumping out of his chair and moving toward the bed.

I wondered how much Jack was into it for. When he started in with that stuff, there had to be *plenty* because a lot was never enough.

Gibby said, "Don't I get a kiss?"

I could feel the Smith & Wesson pressing against my rib cage and for a minute thought about giving Gibby the old Wyatt Earp. Not that I didn't like him. He had his good points to be sure. But at that moment I couldn't think of what they were. He was enormous, not fat, just big, and had hair like a husky.

The thing that killed me was, Jack considered Gibby a true friend. My position was, friends don't sell you coke and push you further into debt. And by the way, what the *fuck*? You're going into *debt* to buy *coke*? Ah *hem* . . . I could be pretty holier than thou, but god*damn*. It really ate me up. There I was, weighing out whether I had enough money to pay for the luxury of half-and-half in our coffee for Christ's sake, and Jack's off going in on eightballs with his pals.

Speed was pulling rifles out from under the bed. "Jack and I can handle it, Speed," I called.

"Oh, you think so? You take a look at your boyfriend yet? I don't think he'll be handling *much*."

"Shut the fuck up, Speed, I'm fine."

I studied Jack's face, which admittedly looked a little off, while he repeated, "I'm fine, I'm totally fine, Betty, I swear."

"So if you don't want to be the one doing that deer yourself, I suggest you leave it to the professional," Speed said, taking control of the situation.

"All right. But I'm driving. Let's go."

The four of us squeezed into the front seat like a family of Gypsies. Snow was coming down even harder now, if that was possible, and I worried I wouldn't be able to locate the deer. I'd use the trailer park as a guide. I was driving faster than I should have been, but we'd already wasted enough time.

"Hey, leadfoot Lizzy, careful," Gibby said, lighting up a joint and passing it over to Speed. "You don't wanna hit a *deer*."

"You roll this with your ass, man?" Speed asked as we passed the trailer park.

Taking my eyes off the road a split second, I looked over

and saw each of them holding a rifle, nozzle up between his knees. Making out her form in the distance, I pumped the brakes. "Pull over and cut the lights," Speed said. "It's not the season, and I don't wanna give any of those fish and game jokers anything to complain about. We're not gonna let this baby go to waste."

"I'll go out there withya. For moral support," Gibby said, rubbing his hands up and down the barrel of the rifle with a little too much gusto.

Those coked-up bastards shooting the deer up like a piñata was one thing I did not want to see.

"I'll take care of it, Speed," said Jack, perhaps thinking the same thing.

"Seriously, man," Speed said, "I'll even dress her down forya, not to worry."

I saw the deer, hanging upside down from a tree, Speed standing beside her in a blood-soaked apron, Buck knife in hand. "Shut up," I said, pulling the .357 out of my pocket.

"Giddyup," Gibby said, out of the corner of his mouth.

"Shit, darlin', you sure you know what you're doing with that thing?" Speed asked.

"Shit yeah, she knows what she's doing," Jack said. He'd been taking me out in the woods for target practice, and I was a pretty decent shot. I'd been on the riflery team at camp.

"You all stay here," I said.

Jack said, "I'll come with you."

"I'd like to do it alone, Jack, if you don't mind."

"All right, Betty," Jack said. His tone was straightforward. He'd let me do what I had to. "We'll wait here."

Speed harrumphed, and before slamming the door I heard Gibby say, "When'd you turn into a feminist, dude?"

Kneeling down next to the deer, I ran a hand over her warm fur for the second time that night, feeling the shallow in and out of her breath. "It's all right, girl. It's all going to be over soon."

The gunmetal was warm from my inside pocket. Thumbing back the hammer, I held the barrel at her temple with two hands, just beside her eye. For an instant, I imagined I could see her looking at me. It was too dark though.

A blast boomed across the valley as the .357 kicked back, causing the gun to jump slightly. I could already feel the jolt of adrenaline subside in the dark, empty pit of my stomach as I watched the blood soak the snow under her head and fan out into a warm pool beneath my knees. This time, when I touched her, there was nothing.

I knelt there for a while, praying in my own lame-ass way— asking God to take care of her up in heaven. For some reason, I couldn't stop thinking about Rudolph the Red-Nosed Rein-deer, and how sad I used to get as a kid watching that show. Until the end, anyway, when everything turns out great.

After the blast and the echo, the silence was deafening, as they say. I heard the car long before I saw the lights, which by the time I stood, was bearing down in the distance. *Good Christ Almighty.*

"All right, the service is over." Speed had already grabbed the deer's hind legs and was attempting to drag her off the road. Jack and Gibby joined in, and together they managed to lug her off to the side. "Betty, get in the truck and drive."

I drove about a mile up the road before pulling a U-y right there on Highway 89 and heading for home.

chapter **10**

The first thing that didn't look right was the chartreuse Volkswagen Beetle parked in our spot. The second thing that had us scratching our heads was the cabin, lit up like a Christmas tree.

"Whose car is *that*," I said, more a statement than a question.

"Could be one of the Kids," Speed said. The cabin next to his was home to five snowboarders from Cincinnati, who worked various kitchen prep and sales clerk jobs. They were all just out of high school, so we called them the Kids.

"Betty, did you leave all those lights on?" Jack chided.

"Nuh-uh."

"Dude, did I leave my duffel in your kitchen?" Gibby asked, sounding slightly frantic.

"I left your duffel in my kitchen," Jack said.

We all got out of the truck and headed down the boot path. "*Dude*, if anyone fucked with my stuff . . ."

"How much *stuff* was there?" I asked.

"Quite a bit," Jack said.

"Terrific," I said, my voice rising as we got to the door. "And who was this *stuff* for?"

"Betty, we'll talk about it later."

"No, Jack. I don't want to talk about it later, I'd like to talk about it right *now*, if you don't mind."

"Look, Betty, don't get mad at him," Gibby said. "It's my stuff. For me."

"Fuck off, Gibby. No offense," I said, flinging myself against the door. I was in no mood for any cockamamie excuses. If Jack was planning on spending our gas and grocery money on coke, I damn well wanted to know about it.

"Wail, wail, *wail*. Eef eet eesn't deh, how do you say? Deh *homewrecker, dehhhh, husband snatcher*? Mon *Dieu*, what appened to your pantalon?"

I was so startled by the sight of Muriel at the kitchen table that I actually felt my chin drop. The dim orange glow of a single lightbulb shined directly over her thick blond hair hanging in Swiss Miss pigtails, one side dyed green. She was the kind of girl who could get away with dyeing her hair like that and still look fabulous with those outdoorsy Nordic features—large blue eyes, perfect straight nose, and a creamy complexion that had turned mocha from the sun. From a clear glass, she sipped something that looked like water but which I knew was probably vodka.

I must have looked like Lizzie Borden by comparison.

"Did you finally keel im? Ah?"

Looking down at the dark red circles on my pants, all I could think was that if I didn't get them into some water soon, my favorite jeans were going to be ruined. I must have been in shock.

"Muriel, what are you doing here?" Jack asked, stepping past me.

"De ghost of cheaders past!" she exclaimed. "I followed Gibby from Salt Lake. Where we used to live together, remember? Ah?" Muriel's accent waxed and waned, in relative sync with her emotions.

"You didn't happen to find a green duffel in here anywhere?" Gibby asked from the open door.

"De one wit all de white powder een it?"

"Close the door," Jack said. Boy, did he look pissed.

"I'll just be taking my bag and heading over to Speed's if you don't mind," Gibby said, trying to sound as casual as a customer in a checkout line.

"Een de reever."

"Excuse me?" Gibby asked, leaning forward, cocking his head.

"I trew your sheet een de reever, Coke Chef. You should tank me I deedn't call de cops."

"Tell me you're just fucking with me, Muriel," Gibby said, his ruddy face going pale.

"If you'll excuse me," I said, "I'm going to change my pants." As I headed for the bathroom, Muriel's tirade of "putains" and "de la merdes," Gibby's "Stupid frog bitches" and "motherfuckers," receded behind me.

Stripping off the blood-soaked jeans, I stuck a rubber stopper in the drain, got the Woolite out from underneath the sink, and ran the water as hard as it would go, attempting to drown out the mayhem. The sink was so small, the water sprayed out onto the floor as I scrunched the jeans in there.

I'd only met Muriel once, over a year ago, down at a party in Salt Lake, where she ran a health-food store. About a week after Jack and I first slept together. In their apartment. In their bed. I know, I know . . . it was to be, as Jack called it, "our little secret." It sounds worse than it felt at the time. Believe me.

Afterward, I got so Swiss on the bed, that it must have been a dead giveaway. Any wife that comes home to hospital corners like those is going to start asking questions.

So we were all down at this party in Salt Lake when Muriel dragged me into the kitchen. She was pretty drunk by then. Her cheeks flushed, a festering cold sore shining with ointment on her lip. She got right to the point. "I sink my husband's een love wis you" is what she said.

Clearly, after our rendezvous at their apartment, I knew he *liked* me.

"You wanna know why?" she asked.

Before I could reply she turned and squeezed a hunk of her jeaned thigh. "I'm fat. And old. He is, how do you say, *il en a marre de moi.*" She was trying to summon the words. "He's tired of me."

She was twenty-six and, as I've already said, quite lovely, there was no denying it. She might have been feeling a little less-than because of the cold sore, but hey. She made it sound like she was on the turbo train to Jenny Craig. I couldn't think

of a single guy I knew who'd have kicked her out of bed for eating crackers.

I waved her off, smiling this sort of don't-be-ridiculous,
smile.

"Here," she said, grabbing my hand and pressing it to the
side of her ass. "Feel."

"Firm," I said. And it was too.

I mean there you are in a stranger's kitchen fondling your
lover's wife's ass, and because it's happening to you, in real
time, it almost seems normal.

"Used to be," she slurred, taking another gulp off her Beck's.
"When I was your age, I looked good too."

Strictly the rantings of a drunken foreigner. I am tall, which
goes a long way in the realm of weight distribution. I had on
one of those Brooks Brothers no-iron button-downs with a pair
of stretchy black hip-huggers, which looked okay I guess.
Maybe even, as she said, good. I'm not going to lie out of some
kind of false modesty and say I think I'm a dog or anything.

"Look at me," she demanded.

"You're very beautiful," I said. And I meant it.

Holding the back of her hand up to the side of her mouth,
she whispered, "My husband's a wanderful luhver, you know.
You should sleep wit im."

Sweet Jesus.

"Seriously, I give you permission. Go ahead, I don mine."

"Muriel?"

It was Jack, come to the kitchen to get the 411.

"Go ahead!" she screamed, "sleep wit er, see if I care!"

"Muriel, calm down," Jack said, taking her by the arm, and

leading her to the sink, presumably to have a quiet word. I could hear him trying to talk her down, but it was as effective as a toreador trying to soothe a bull.

"Don you tell me to be quiet! Dare she is! Fucker!"

I couldn't tell if she meant *fuck* her, fuck *her*, that Jack was a fucker, or all three. But that was my cue to get the hell out of there.

"Cochon!" Muriel shouted, a glass shattering against what I hoped wasn't my coveted pink fridge. If she was going to start breaking shit, she would have to leave.

I was sitting on the toilet, my pounding head in my hands. To top everything off, I sensed that familiar yeasty itch coming on, and there wasn't a tube of Monistat in the house. Doing the "wipe and scratch," I became muddleheaded as to what the proper attire might be for kicking my boyfriend's wife out of the house. I didn't want to look like I'd tried too hard, but it seemed necessary to at least appear to be an improvement over one's opponent. Not that I was in any mood for debating such matters. Or considered her a threat.

Out in the main room, I hunted through the cabinet drawers in a towel. "You wanna divorce? Sure! Pas de problem! Ruin my life why don't you! I don luff you anymore! I hate you! Do you hear me? I can't stand de sight of you!" She sobbed.

By that time Jack had stopped talking, his standard method for dealing with drama.

I'm a complete sucker for tears. Probably because of my mother. In a way, Muriel sort of reminded me of her.

Selecting a fitted turtleneck and a nicely worn pair of jeans, I put on a pair of wool socks, slipped on a pair of Birkenstocks, and walked into the kitchen.

Muriel was hunched over the table, stripped down to a Fruit of the Loom wife beater, scratch marks (self-inflicted, I was sure) swelling on her arms.

Jack was standing, his back against the door, staring stony eyed off into space.

"What the hell, Muriel?" I asked, pulling over a chair and putting my arm around her shoulder. She didn't try too hard to shrug it off, so I left it there. "Jack, maybe you should leave us for a minute?"

"Be my guest," he said, putting his hat back on, kicking open the door.

Once the cold blast had receded, Muriel sniffled a couple of times. "Why deed you do eet?" she asked. "You knew he was married, why deedn't you leave eem alone?"

"Do you need a drink?" I asked, smelling full well that she didn't, as I made my way to the fridge. We could barely afford to eat, but by God, there was always a bottle of Absolut at the ready in the freezer. No one could say we didn't have our priorities. And right now, pouring myself a stiff one was at the top of my list.

"Do you have red wine?" she asked.

"Sorry. We've got beer, vodka, and Squirt."

"What ees dees, Squirt?"

"It's sort of a lemony type soda. Should I pour you some?"

"Ees naturel?"

Its Day-Glo yellow coloring pretty much excluded Squirt

from the realm of *naturel*. "I'm not sure if it's natural. It's pretty tasty though. Would you like to try it?"

"Ya, sure," she said, waving her hand away to show she'd already sunk this low, why not? "Wheat vodka, *s'il te plait*."

"You want ice?" You never knew with these Frenchies.

She nodded.

Pouring our drinks, I said, "You should put some Neosporin on those scratches."

"Oh, wadda you care!" she cried.

"I'm sorry about what happened. But you should know, I left Utah so that you two could work things out," I said, putting her drink down in front of her.

"I see. Ees dat your *super* technique? You *bez* eem, den leave eem to me? Parfait!"

"Muriel, maybe it's not for me to say, but didn't you *both* cheat?"

"De beegest mistake I make ees taking our marriage seriously. I had to see for myself. He doesn't luff me anymore. May I smoke?"

"Sure."

Fishing through her bag on the floor, she pulled out a packet of Drum tobacco and started rolling. When she was finished, she held it out to me and asked, "You want?"

I shook my head and took a long cold sip of vodka, felt it go warm down into my stomach. I imagined it cleaning out whatever bug had lodged itself inside me. I was in no shape. Physically or emotionally. I hated to admit it, but I kind of liked Muriel. I could relate to her. If all of this nonsense hadn't happened between us, we might have been friends.

"*Du feu?*" she asked motioning with her thumb.

I stared at her uncomprehending.

"You have a light?"

There were Bic lighters in every nook and cranny all over the cabin, but for some reason, there wasn't one in the usual place on the kitchen windowsill. Inside the silverware drawer, I found three. Pulling out a small pink one, I lit the end of her cigarette.

"You remember one teeng," she said, her eyes boring into mine as she picked a piece of tobacco off her lip, "What goes eh-round, comes eh-round."

I hated when people said that. Mostly because I wanted to believe it wasn't true. "Are you speaking from experience, or what?"

She was about to respond when there was a knock at the door.

"Who's knocking?" I said. That's when I noticed the flashing red lights through the kitchen window. "Mother *fuck*. It's the cops."

"Voilà," Muriel said, illustrating her point.

chapter 11

A man in uniform stood in the doorway, one hand on his hip, the other touching the brim of his hat. "Sorry to bother you, ma'am, but we got a report of a gun blast up the road by the trailer park, and I'm down here checking it out."

His timing couldn't have been worse. Or better, depending on your point of view.

"Come in, Officer." I had a be-nice-to-cops policy. One that had been put into effect for various vehicular missteps—speeding, passing on the double yellow, stuff like that. In my limited experience, those fellas really seemed to like it when you kissed their ass.

Walking into the kitchen, he took off his hat and, using it as a pointer, said, "Nice fridge. Got one similar to it."

"Can I offer you something? A glass of water? Coffee?" I may have been going a bit overboard. I didn't want to marry the guy.

"No thanks," he said. "You ladies been here all night?" He looked pretty young and innocent for an officer of the law, clean shaven with a crew cut.

Muriel looked like she'd been fighting with a bobcat.

"Mind me asking how you got those scratches?"

My heart was pounding so hard I could barely hear Muriel when she looked at me all bewildered and said, *"Pardon? Je ne comprend pas."*

Oh, thank heavens.

"She doesn't speak English," I explained, wondering how much time you could get for lying. Then, moving in closer, "She's got some problems. Mental," I said, my eyes shifting sideways slightly in a show of decorum.

Muriel was going along, smoking her Drum, drinking her Squirt cooler, as though we were just a couple of gals taking a ciggy break.

"That's not wacky tabacky is it?" the cop asked, suddenly reminding me of the Classico jars in the cabinet three feet away. "To be honest," he said, smiling, "I wouldn't know that stuff if it was staring me in the face."

"Me *neither*," I said, going for a look halfway between bewildered and appalled. "No. She rolls her own cigarettes. It's a French thing." I was just guessing, but I had a hunch the good officer had never set foot out of Teton County.

He pressed his lips together and nodded, as though that, indeed, explained everything. "You mind if I take a quick look around?"

"I don't mind at all," I said.

"Eee would care for un peu de spaghetti peut-être?" Muriel asked.

"She talkin' about now?" the officer asked, as if Muriel was from another planet.

"Il aimerai de la sauce de tomats?" Muriel called after us as I led him into the main room.

You could change women without changing the location of your stash I guess. I was wondering how far she would take it when I heard her humming "White Lines."

"My sister went a little nuts one time," the officer said, "so I know how it is. We got her some pills. She's all set now."

"They really do make a pill for everything these days, don't they?" I said. "By the way, aren't you supposed to have a search warrant or something?" I asked, as though it was just an after-thought, a friendly question posed by an innocent, fascinated with the ins and outs of the legal system. "I'm a big fan of *Law & Order*," I added.

"Technically, yes. That's correct," he said, scanning the place. "But if you say it's okay, then it's okay, right?"

"Absolutely," I said, following him toward the bathroom, where my jeans were swimming in a bloody pool.

"I've got a few personals soaking in there," I said. "That time of the month."

"Ho!" he said, glancing at the sink, holding up his hand and turning. "Too much information!"

"I had a little accident."

"Ma'am, you really don't have to go into it. I'm married my-self. I understand." He was checking out the open closet setup, the Marmot shell with the .357 in the inside pocket hanging in between my one summer dress and Jack's flannels. The gun was legally registered, and just about everyone and his brother out there had one, but still. Given the circumstances, it wouldn't look good.

"What the hell's going on in here?"

Jack.

"Your missus here said I could take a look around," the cop said, sounding, I was surprised to hear, slightly nervous.

"Well, last time I checked the *Constitution*, it said that guys like you weren't allowed to do that sort of thing without proper permission. You got proper permission?"

This backwoods survivalist persona was a side of Jack you rarely saw. He was, as most people in Jackson were, of the right-to-bear-arms persuasion. This was, after all, the Wild West. People took their personal property seriously. I knew a cyclist who rode with a handgun strapped to the bottom of his bicycle seat just in case he got harassed for trespassing.

"Look. Don't give me a hard time, sir," the cop said, looking slightly flustered. "I just started this job a week ago."

"That what they tell you to say when you're doing *illegal* searches?" Jack asked.

"I was just taking a quick look around," he said.

"Well, you're done now," Jack said, standing motionless.

I gave the officer a shrug. Work a little good cop, bad cop on him.

"Yee-up, I should probably be gettin' along now," he said, giving me a wink just to let me know it was his idea.

When he'd gone, Jack shook his head and turned to me.

"Betty? You never let a cop look around unless he's got a search warrant."

"Gee, sorry, Jack, maybe I was too preoccupied with your *wife*."

"Look, I'm sorry," he said, putting his hand on my arm. "It's just that, all he had to do was open the kitchen cabinet. . . . I'm not planning on going to jail anytime soon."

"It's okay," I said, wondering how I'd become the kind of girl who needed to be paranoid of cops. Muriel had disappeared. "Where did she go?"

"I think she's crashed."

"Where?"

"On the bed."

"Great."

"We could probably stay over at Speed's. He's got a pullout couch."

"Isn't that where Gibby is?"

"He's on the floor. Hey, why don't we haul the mattress out of the truck and sleep on that?"

Too tired to argue, I went and got my coat.

In the morning, Muriel and Jack were gone. Throwing the down comforter back, I sat up fast, then laid back down. My head was killing me and my crotch itched like a sonofabitch. Where were they? Was this it? *The end?*

Gibby made a noisy entrance. "Anyone up for venny and eggs this morning? Betty? How about a taste of your kill?" he asked, wiping his nose hastily with the back of his finger.

"Where's Jack?" I asked, unable to move. My frontal lobe felt like someone had taken a jackhammer to it.

"Over with Speed."

"What's he doing over there?"

"I'm not at liberty to say."

"You found your duffel."

"In the backseat of Muriel's car. Before she took off," Gibby said, pretending the fireplace was the most interesting thing he'd ever seen. "But listen, Jack sent me over to cook you breakfast."

"Will you do me a favor and please go over and get him? Tell him I'm not feeling so hot."

"Whatsa matter?"

"I don't know. Flu I think."

"Dude, that blows," he said, edgy now to get back over to Speed's and resume Hoovering. "Sit tight!"

I tried to sit up again, and colorful dark patches fluttered before my eyes. Could I actually *see* the synapses spurting chemicals in my brain? I hadn't felt so bad since puking up corn kernels and peas at Suzy Slockbuer's Halloween birthday bash when I was a kid.

Jack was lucky I felt so crappy. It totally derailed the ass whooping he was due for. We'd had a couple of fights over his cocaine consumption before, and they'd always ended in the predictably melodramatic ways—me threatening to leave, him weeping, promising never to do it again. It just made the whole episode with Gibby that much more offensive. Like, obviously he didn't care if I left, didn't think I actually would, or really couldn't help himself. As far as multiple choice answers went, I would have preferred none-of-the-above.

The more I thought about it, the angrier I got. And the angrier I got, the more energetic I became. Swinging my legs off the side of the mattress, I sat with my head in my hands for several seconds before pushing up into the standing position. Jack's footsteps crunched in the snow toward the cabin. By then I'd decided I didn't really feel like seeing him after all.

Making my way over to the armchair, I sat down on a pile of clothes and began sticking my legs into a pair of jeans.

"Betty?" Jack was standing in the doorway between the kitchen and the main room.

"I'm going to the health clinic," I said, without looking at him. I'd never been to a "clinic" before in my life. Maybe that makes me spoiled or something, I don't know. But for me, the word clinic signified many things. It meant I didn't have health insurance. It meant that all of the privilege I'd been raised with was worthless because I wasn't capable of making a living. It meant that my boyfriend had just gone and made our lives that much more difficult for an overrated coke high. It meant understanding the phrase "beggars can't be choosers," applied to me. And if I had to pinpoint the crappiest part about being poor, it was having no choice.

"I'll take you."

"You go to work. I'll take myself."

"Betty, what's wrong?"

Although I wanted to scream "You're what's wrong!" I managed to keep my wits about me. Blaming Jack for what was essentially my problem wouldn't make me feel any better. Generally, I wasn't inclined toward such levelheadedness, but I was trying to conserve energy. I said, "I think I've got the flu, and my crotch is a dog's breakfast. I need some medicine."

"Your crotch? What's the matter with your crotch?"

"Yeah, God forbid anything's wrong with my *crotch*. I have a yeast infection."

"Don't you have some of that cream?"

"No. And it doesn't work anymore anyways. I need a prescription."

"Are you okay to drive?"

"Yeah. I'll try not to hit any more deer."

chapter 12

The waiting room at the Jackson Hole Health Clinic was packed
with Hispanic men, women, and children, taking turns cough-
ing, sneezing, and crying. There were no more seats available,
so I stood propped up against the wall for a while until the father of one of the kids came over and motioned for me to take
his seat. "Muchas gracias," I said.

He smiled and said, "De nada."

Not a minute too soon, boy. I was seriously about to pass
out. I tried to be cool though, smiling at the kids. A little boy
came up to me with one of the children's books they kept there
in the waiting room. It was called something like *A Week of Sun-
days*. There was a big, weird-looking ice cream sundae on the
cover, with little green frogs and brown beetles and stuff sprinkled on top of it. I felt kind of sorry for him because I could tell
he probably didn't get to read too much at home. At least not

in English. He sort of held the book out, like he wanted to show it to me.

A trickle of cold sweat ran down the side of my face. "Would you like me to read it to you?"

He didn't say anything. Just smiled. I didn't know if he was too young to understand me, or maybe he did. He put the book on my lap.

Opening it up, I held the book around right side up for him to see, and read, while he pointed to the frog and beetle sprinkles, cartoon whipped cream and Maraschino cherries. His mother smiled at us from across the room. I liked reading to the little boy. It helped take my mind off the itch.

After about two hours of waiting, the nurse finally called, "Elizabeth Winters?"

"Here!" I practically screamed.

"Follow me."

She led me into an examination room, told me to take off everything, put on a gown. The doctor would be in momentarily.

In my experience, the doctor is never in *momentarily*. But I'd been waiting two long hours, what was another fifteen minutes? Half an hour? I really hate waiting in those examination rooms, because by the time you get in there, you're so optimistic that the doctor's going to see you any minute you never remember to bring the magazine you were reading from the waiting room. So instead of distracting yourself with a *Good Housekeeping* or *People* or something, you're stuck naked on that table, checking out the medical paraphernalia—serums, lotions, lubricants, swabs, bandages, what have you—working yourself into a lather about if and how the doctor will use those things on you.

There was a quick rap on the door, and after I said, "Come in," a youngish man holding a folder, wearing a purple pile jacket, jeans, and a pair of hiking boots entered. He looked like your typical superfit, raccoon-tanned Jacksonite, except he wore a pair of silver wire-rimmed glasses, which made him appear slightly more academic. "Hi," he said, holding out his hand.

"Please tell me you're the nurse," I said. He was a little too good-looking to be the sort of fellow you'd want rooting around your privates.

"I'm Dr. Wright. The nurse will be in in a moment."

"I'm Elizabeth Winters. Betty," I said, and we shook.

"Winters. Is your father a member of the New Canaan Historical Society by any chance?"

My father was so out of context in that environment, I hardly knew how to respond. "Yes," I said, thinking now might be a good time to run.

"I remember the name from some of those monthly newsletters they send out."

"So you're a member?"

"Used to be when I lived there. My parents still are."

"That's nice," I said, realizing how disingenuous it sounded as soon as it came out.

Turning to face me, he said, "You know everything that happens in this office is private. I don't want you to worry about it." His large, brown eyes bore into mine.

"I'm not worried," I said. Part of me was actually pleasantly surprised. I mean, I wasn't expecting to get New Canaan service in a *clinic*. "What brings you here?" I wanted to know.

"I like to ski," he said, flipping through the folder. "So, it says here you've been suffering from headaches? Muscle pain?"

"That's correct," I said. *Keep it light. Keep it clinical.*

The nurse came in and began straightening up the items around the sink before standing quietly in the corner like a sentry.

He checked my eyes, tapped my back, poked my armpit nodes, caressed my throat glands, peered into my ears with a light, then stuck a thermometer in one.

"Neat," I said, as it beeped.

"Well," he said. "You have a slight fever. Just over a hundred. Nothing serious. Your glands are a little swollen. I'm inclined to think you've got a flu bug of some sort."

I was praying he wouldn't mention the "vaginal itching" I'd also specified under "symptoms." It was like playing doctor with a slightly older version of Jake Gyllenhaal. Pretty much the *last* guy I'd want seeing my ho-ho in that condition.

"I understand you also have some itching?" he asked. He was a gynecologist after all.

"Um, yes," I said. "I've been experiencing some itching."

Sliding a cushioned stool with wheels over to the table, he pulled the stirrups out from the sides. "Put your heels up in here, and scootch your butt forward."

This guy doesn't mess around. "I get yeast infections a lot," I ventured.

"Well, let's take a look and see what we find," he said, shining the swivel light in between my legs and putting on a pair of rubber gloves. A piece of his bangs fell onto his forehead.

I tried to pretend he was older, much, and covered with carbuncles, but it wasn't helping.

"Mmm-hmm. Looks like you've got a yeast infection all right."

"How about some Diflucan?" I blurted. *That's it, Betty, impress him with your yeast-remedy know-how.*

Pushing the stool back with an amused expression, he said, "Diflucan it is," and began writing the prescription. "You can take sitz baths . . ."

"I only have a shower," I said, sitting up and pulling the sheet primly back over my thighs. *Just hand that prescription over and I'll be on my way.*

"Showers are fine too."

The good doctor was taking it all in stride, handling the situation like a real champ. Very professional. Very removed.

"When you're run-down, not getting enough sleep, you become prone to this sort of thing. So my advice to you is"—and here he finished writing and gave me the Gyllenhaal smile—"take it easy."

Luckily, the girl at the pharmacy didn't make me feel like a complete jackass for not having health insurance, because that Diflucan wasn't cheap. One tiny pill nearly cleared out my wallet. It looked like everyone would be getting my famous orange-cranberry-nut bread for Christmas. It's a major hit with the old friends and family. At least everyone *pretends* to like it.

Since my afternoon lesson was shot, I decided to stop by Albertson's to pick up a bag of frozen cranberries and the zesting orange. My family wasn't too big on Christmas anyway. Mom's usually the only one doling out presents—oversized turtlenecks from Charter Club mostly, that she buys on sale at JCPenney.

Gift giving is such a rare talent. I never know what to get for people. It's almost like a phobia—gift-giving anxiety or something. Because it's not like I don't think about it. In fact, I *over*think about it. So I'll get someone something I might like. Which isn't really the spirit of the whole thing. It's supposed to be more about what the *other* person likes.

The thing is, I should know from experience that people aren't too picky. I mean, I can be happy with a bar of soap. It's not like you have to go out and buy someone a car or anything.

chapter 13

The look on my parents' faces when they stepped through the threshold of the cabin was one of sheer desperation. "It's so dark" was the first thing Mom said.

"It's cool," Benny said, surveying the place.

I'd been napping.

"How's my girl?" Dad said, putting on a brave face as they approached.

"A little better," I said.

"You've been to the doctor?" Mom asked.

"Yes." I'd missed an elegant Christmas dinner at the Range. In some ways being sick was a major relief. It kept me from having to juggle everyone. "Would anyone care for some tea or hot chocolate or something?" I asked, getting out of the bed, walking toward the kitchen. "I'm sorry, I wasn't expecting you guys so soon."

"Elizabeth, dear, why are you walking that way?"

"Pulled a muscle," I said. "Hazard of the job."

"What is it, your leg?"

"Hamstring," I said. "Sit down, make yourselves at home."

"Some *home*," Mom said.

I made lots of noise pretending to be busy in the kitchen, setting four nonmatching mugs, a teapot filled with hot water, a box of Domino sugar, an assortment of loose tea bags, instant cocoa, and a chipped trout-shaped creamer filled with milk on a tray.

The three of them were sitting on the couch in an uncomfortable looking row when I returned and delicately placed the tray on the imitation-wood coffee table.

"How lovely," Mom said, looking ready to burst into tears. She had on a pair of those furry boots that bunnies like Charlene wore, with suede pants tucked in. Her face indicated a recent refresher at the dermatologist.

"I'll have hot chocolate," Benny said.

"Help yourself, big guy," I said, handing him a packet of cocoa.

"Dad? What'll it be? Earl Grey? Constant Comment? Or plain old Lipton." Dad wore a pair of olive wide-wales from L.L.Bean, a yellow oxford poking out from beneath a charcoal gray cashmere V-neck. His long legs were scrunched uncomfortably behind the table. "Here, let me pull this out for you," I said, bending to reposition it.

"Oh, I almost forgot," Mom said, "I brought presents."

"She made us wait," Benny said.

"I wanted us all to be together when we opened our gifts,"

she said, reaching into a large brown JCPenney bag and pulling out three nicely wrapped rectangular boxes.

The expression on Mom's face when I reached under the bed and presented the orange-cranberry-nut bread made me glad I'd made the effort.

"Is this your special bread?" Mom asked, sniffing the foil. "Thank you, I'm going to have some with my tea."

Parents can make you feel like a winner for the smallest efforts sometimes.

Not to be outdone, Benny dug into his pocket and pulled out a wad of crumpled money. "Two-dollar bills!" he said, smiling. "One for everyone. They're good luck, you know."

"Benny, how sweet," Mom said, taking her two-dollar bill and folding it into her wallet. "I'm going to hold on to this."

Benny winked at me.

"Go on, Elizabeth, open your gift," Mom said.

Ripping off the Christmas tree wrapping, I dug through the tissue. "What's this?" I asked, pulling out a large, red leather pocketbook. "Wow," I said. "This is really beautiful." It was the most amazing bag I'd ever seen, one of those superexpensive Coach deals that were all the rage back in Manhattan. I didn't want to appear ungrateful, but what the hell was I going to do in Jackson, Wyoming, with that? "Thanks, Mom. I won't kiss you. You don't want to catch what I have."

"Moowa," she said, pressing her hand to her lips and blowing.

"Hey, thanks, Mom!" Benny said, holding up a new Patagonia pile jacket.

Now a jacket like that, I could have used.

Anyway.

Looking over at Dad, Benny asked, "What did you get, Pops?" Dad hadn't opened his gift or uttered a word since I'd come in from the kitchen.

"Why do you have a gun on your bedside table?" he asked quietly, staring into his mug.

"Oh, that? That's Jack's. He likes to keep it there for protection," I said, real casual-like.

"I hope it's not loaded," Dad said, stirring in a teaspoon of sugar.

"Um. Actually," I said, calm as could be, "Jack's motto is, if it's not loaded why bother?" I didn't push it with the carefree chuckle.

"Well then, he's a bigger idiot than I thought."

"He's not an idiot," I said. "Everyone has guns out here, Dad." As soon as the words came out, I realized how silly and defensive I sounded.

"You're not *everyone*," Mom broke in. She'd turned the corner. The Christmas cheer was over, the third degree had begun. "You're our daughter."

Looking back on it, I can see where they were coming from, I really can. At the time though, I was in no shape to appreciate their concern.

"Ida," Dad comforted, patting her knee.

"Come on, you guys, lighten up," Benny said. "You know how to shoot that thing, right?"

"Of course."

"It makes no difference," Dad said. "Having a loaded gun in the house, in *plain view*, no less, is an invitation for disaster."

"All you have to do is watch *Unsolved Mysteries*," Mom said.

"Do you all mind if I lay down for a minute? I'm not feeling so hot," I said, closing my eyes and putting the back of my arm over my forehead like a lady in distress. I never should have agreed to let them come. It was very bad timing.

"What happens if you get into a fight, and one of you decides to use that thing?" Dad asked, sitting forward, his forearms on his knees.

"That's not going to happen," I said in monotone, almost adding that we weren't a couple of rednecks. Given our present circumstances, however, I thought better of it.

Mom got up from the couch and went into the kitchen. When she came back she had a bottle of Old Style in her hand. "I'm so parched," she said.

"Why don't you have a glass of water then, Ida, honey? You're probably suffering from the altitude."

"This is perfect, dear. Very quenching," she said, gulping down half the bottle. "The altitude is the *least* of my worries right now. Sweetheart? Are you listening to me?"

"Yes, Mom."

"I want to know whether you've been thinking at *all* about your future."

A hot surge bolted to my chest. When *wasn't* I thinking about it was more to the point. "One day at a time, right?" I said, trying to deflect, and, who knows, maybe provoke a little too.

"Good attitude," Mom shot back sarcastically.

I wasn't going to bother telling her about Pete Laurey. Extreme skiing was hardly what she'd consider a life. No, people

needed to have plans in place, walk a straight path, set attain-
able goals, make (or, in her case, marry) buttloads of cash.

"Hey." It was Benny, standing by the bathroom door. "What
are you doing with this?" he asked, shaking a vial of pills. "My
roommate takes this stuff."

Mom's face went white. "What are *those*? Narcotics?"

"It's not *drugs*, Mom," Benny said, before I could answer,
"it's this stuff for herpes."

"I beg your *pardon*?" Mom said, cocking her head forward.

"One more thing to recommend this Jack character," Dad
said.

Oy *vay*. I had never seen the bottle before but suspected it
had been left behind by she of the cold sores. It made me so fu-
rious that Dad was forming some slimy judgment about Jack,
who by the way, he'd never met, that I sat up and said, "It's not
Jack's."

"What do you mean?" Mom said. "It's not—"

"It's mine." Let them think what they wanted.

Benny backpedaled. "You know, for cold sores and stuff."

Drinking down the rest of the beer, Mom burped delicately.
No one spoke. Dad looked as heartbroken and generally for-
lorn as I'd ever seen him. "Hey," Benny said, breaking the ice,
"can I check out the gun?"

"Sure," I said, relieved for the change of subject. "Just be
careful not to point it at anyone."

Removing the .357 from its leather holster, he sat feeling its
weight. "It's heavy," he said.

"Benny, put that away," Mom said.

"Have you ever seen one of these up close before?" he asked, squinting one eye shut, lining up the finder, and inadvertently letting the gun's muzzle drop in her direction.

"Don't point the gun at anything you don't want to kill," I said.

"Whoops. Sorry," he said, lining up another shot.

"I wish you wouldn't mess around with that thing," Dad said.

"But, Dad, you have one, don't you? That old one from Uncle Leo?"

"That's more of a keepsake," Dad said.

"You two need to chill out," Benny said.

"Here, hand it over," I said, reaching my arm out. I meant to take out the bullets.

"Hold up," he said, fiddling with the hammer.

The noise of the blast was so shocking it felt almost like being in another time zone, where there was no sound at all. Except there was, and it was loud as hell, causing the four of us to jump simultaneously.

The bullet had entered the mattress, approximately three inches from my left toe.

The smoke from the explosion hovered between us as the feathers from the down comforter lazily came to rest. "Holy shit!" Benny finally announced, shaking out his hand. "Are you okay?"

"I think so," I said, wiggling my toes to be sure. "Is everyone else all right?"

"Ida?" Dad asked.

Mom looked at him wild-eyed, shaking her head in disbelief.

"Answer me, Ida, yes or no?" he said, speaking slowly, leaning in toward her.

"Yes, yes, I'm fine." The gun blast had subdued her.

"Holy sheeeat," Benny said again, looking at his hand. That fucking killed."

My parents didn't bother calling him on the language. Apparently, this was the occasion for it.

"What's that called again?" Benny asked, inspecting his forefinger.

"Kickback," I said.

Dropping to his knees, Benny started hunting under the bed. "Where did that fucking thing go? Oh my God, Lizzy, there's a hole in the floor."

"A big hole?"

"Big enough to stick my pinkie through."

"There's some duct tape in the cabinet under the kitchen sink."

"Well, thank God we're all alive," Dad said, grimly.

"Wow," Benny said, coming back into the room with the tape, looking ready either to cry or to burst into hysterical laughter. "I'm really sorry about that. I didn't think I was touching the trigger."

"Famous last words," Dad said.

"Why don't you put it back in its holster?" I said quietly.

No one spoke. It was as if we didn't want to discuss the tragedy that might have been.

"You're going to tape it?" Mom asked.

"Until we get around to renovating," I said.

When she spoke again it was to change the subject. "Will you be able to eat with us tonight?"

"I really don't think I'm up to it," I said. I didn't want to stay sick forever.

"We're leaving in two days."

"I'm sorry I wasn't a better host."

"We could come visit again tomorrow. Bring you some groceries?"

"Jack has the day off," I lied. All I wanted to do was sleep.

Dad was already standing, jittery to get out of Dodge. "I think we'd better say our good-byes now then," he said, running his hand through his thick gray hair. For him, I knew, there was nothing left to say.

Coming over to the bed one by one, they kissed me, like I was a corpse in a casket.

chapter 14

Because it was down in a valley, the point was somewhat pro-
tected by the wind. For the same reason, it got dark earlier in
the day. There was almost no natural light left in the cabin
when I got up to put the tea stuff away. I hadn't been expecting
the family visit to be a positive experience necessarily, maybe
just a little less of a disaster. The more I fought for my indepen-
dence, the less control over my life I seemed to have. Not that
I'd been such a winner to begin with. It pushed me into a depressing mode of self-examination that my parents might have
appreciated but which wasn't exactly what you'd call produc-
tive. I mean, Frank Sinatra did it "his way," but he knew what
the hell he wanted to do. What could I say I was fighting for—
the right to party?

Pouring the milk from the creamer back into the carton, I
spotted something brown and furry lying on the ground below

the window underneath a small aspen. For a minute I thought the boys had left the deer carcass out where everyone could see it. Then I saw it move.

It was a baby moose. Usually where there was a baby, the mommy wasn't far away. I stood by the window looking down at him for a long time, thinking about the past few days—how upset my parents were, how irrevocably fucked up everything was. And here was this baby moose, huddled next to the cabin, his mother nowhere in sight. "Where's your mama, sweetie?"

He stared up at me. I guess, compared to him, alone in the snowy cold, I couldn't complain. Cutting a slab of cranberry-orange-nut bread with a serrated knife, I toyed with the idea of feeding him some but thought of the story of those numskulls in Yellowstone who'd covered their baby's hand with honey so they could snap a picture of a bear licking it off. That little photo op didn't go exactly as planned.

Breaking off a corner of the slice, I stuck it in my mouth and started to chew. *Damn*, that was some good bread. I must have been starting to feel better, because after downing one slice, I cut off another, popped it in the toaster oven to golden, slathered it with butter, and polished that off too, washing it all down with a glass of cold milk.

Getting back into bed, I tried to read a little *Atlas Shrugged*. I say *tried* because I was doing that thing where your eyes scan the words, but you can't remember what you just read. Maybe my parents were right. I mean, was living here in semisqualor with Jack my destiny? Was I putting my *abilities* to good use? Come to think of it, what *were* my abilities anyway?

The problem with me is, even though Mac *said* I was good enough to be in Pete Laurey's video, I couldn't help thinking she was just blowing smoke up my ass. I wonder if everyone's that way. Like maybe no one really believes they're good enough at anything, but some go ahead and do it anyway.

It was dark outside when Jack walked through the door carrying a stack of wood in his arms. Placing it gently on the stone hearth in front of the fireplace, he quietly piled crumpled up pieces of the *Jackson Hole News* and kindling. Once that got going, he laid three split pieces of log on top. He'd learned how to build the perfect fire as a Boy Scout back in Michigan.

My head was full of cobwebs as I rolled onto my side to face him. Taking off his jacket and boots, he went to the kitchen, opened a beer, came back in, and sat Indian style in front of the flames.

I watched him sitting there for what felt like a long time, wondering if he had any regrets. Rolling over to face the log wall, I closed my eyes and fell back asleep. When I woke up later, Jack was curled up behind me, his arms wrapped around my waist, his face pressed against my shoulder.

That night, Jack mixed up a venison meat loaf, adding ketchup, canned tomatoes, bread crumbs, and dried spices. He'd stopped off at Albertson's for some prewashed salad in a bag. It was the first taste of anything green I'd had in a while. He'd even picked up a bottle of red wine and lit a couple of candles.

"I hope you didn't spend too much," I said. The wine, I happened to know, was in the ten-dollar range.

"Don't worry about it," he said, pouring me a glass. "You need to get better."

"Right. I've just been thinking, are we going to have enough to pay rent this month? With the work I've missed?"

"I said, don't worry about it. To your health," he said, clinking his bottle of Old Style against my glass.

"Wait, what do you mean, don't worry about it?"

"I mean my father just sent me a check."

Jack's father owned a bunch of restaurants in Michigan and was, for all practical purposes, loaded. Like my parents, though, he wasn't into throwing his money around.

"Just like that?" I asked.

"No, Betty, I called him and told him I needed it," he said, tersely. I don't think he was too proud about it.

"Well, that was nice of him."

"Yes, it was. How is it?" he asked, watching me take a bite of the meat loaf.

"Delicious," I said, leaning over to kiss him.

"I'm glad," he said.

We ate in silence then. I was thinking how good it tasted when Jack said, "Muriel called. Our meeting with the INS is the day before the Pete Laurey tryouts."

"So?"

"Well, I don't think it's going to be a problem. I could probably drive back up here the same night. It depends. They might need to see us the next day too. I don't think that's going to happen, but it's a possibility."

"Okay," I said.

"I also spoke with Cardiac, from Morris bike shop?"

"Uh-huh."

"They want me to ride on their team this season."

"Which means?"

"Moving back down to Salt Lake."

Jack had been dreaming of riding in the Tour de France with Lance Armstrong since before I'd met him. He was a strong contender too. Even with all the partying. I'd never seen anyone who could abuse his body the way he did and get up to ride a hundred and twenty miles at dawn. I knew how much bike racing meant to him, but moving back to Salt Lake wasn't a plan I was particularly enthusiastic about. We'd left town for a reason. There was too much bad blood there. The whole purpose of moving up to Jackson had been to start over somewhere new. Away from Muriel, and bad influences like Gibby. Maybe it had been naïve of me to believe that moving somewhere else would erase all the old problems. I suspected ulterior motives, but it wasn't like I could come out dissing his Tour de France dreams. They were the noble part of the argument.

The meat loaf was losing its flavor.

"Betty?"

"What?"

"Aren't you going to say something?"

"Well, Jack, what does that mean? It sounds like you're not really into the whole Pete Laurey thing."

He looked down at his plate and didn't say anything for a while. "I could still try out, but if I made it which is a long shot. . . . I mean it's a long shot for both of us, right?"

"Yeah, it's a long shot, but we *could* make it. Think about how cool that would be."

"They follow the snow to South America for the summer, don't they? Argentina? Chile? I wouldn't be able to race then."

"That's true. But why don't we keep our options open? I mean, what am I supposed to do in Salt Lake City all summer?"

"You could probably work the brunch buffet up at the Buckeye," he said quickly, as though he'd been anticipating that very question.

The thought of being a chafing dish queen all summer made me want to heave. I'd already pretty much decided that the brunch buffet at the Buckeye would not be my lot in life. "That idea doesn't thrill me," I said.

"Look, Betty, I'm not going to tell *you* not to try out. I think you should."

"Well thank you very much," I said.

"Look, if I can make it, I'll try out too, okay?"

"Don't do me any favors."

"I'm not," he said, putting his hand over mine. "We don't have to make any decisions yet."

After dinner, I walked up to the pay phone and gave Lynne a call. "You want to ski Glory tomorrow morning?" I asked.

"Betty, how are you feeling?"

"I'm better," I said, mostly to convince myself.

"Are you coming back to work?"

"Yes, I am."

"You sound a little riled."

"Jack and I had a fight. Sort of."

"You two lovebirds fight? I'm shocked."

"Happens to the best of us."

"Sure, I'd be psyched for Glory," she said. "The backcountry report said the avalanche danger's low. The snow's been a little packed out in the area, but it should be dece on the pass. You sure you're feeling up to it?"

"I've got to start getting back into shape sometime. Might as well go whole hog," I said, figuring attitude was everything.

"I'll meet you at the pass at, what you want to say, six? Six-thirty? Your call."

"Let's make it six."

chapter 15

The Subaru idled while the coffee brewed. Clif bars, Nalgene bottle of Exceed, PIEPS, and shovel spread across the kitchen table. The pins and needles from the showerhead were the perfect wake-up call. It was five o'clock and Jack was asleep. We'd be taking separate cars to work that day.

It was still dark outside as I made my way up the boot path, EMS travel mug in hand, shovel strapped to the back of an old Mountainsmith backpack slung over my shoulder. The snow crunched beneath my boots, each breath freezing another nose hair.

My purple, secondhand Tuas were piled in the back, waiting to be ridden. I had the parabolic downhills, but I still tellied the old way—double black leather Merrell boots and three-pins. It was a little awkward driving in telly boots, what with the rectangular bit of leather sticking out from the toe, but compared to clunky plastic downhills, they felt almost like slippers.

Throwing the pack in back with the skis, I scraped the ice off the windshield, back window, and headlights, threw myself into the driver's seat, and headed for the pass.

There is a small parking area between Wilson, Wyoming, and Victor, Idaho, where anyone can park, hike, and ski. For free. You've got to either skin up (skins are synthetic strips of animal-like fur that attach to the bottoms of your skis to give uphill traction) or, in the case of Glory Bowl, follow the boot track. It was 6:45 by the time we'd parked and strapped our skis on either side of our backpacks, shovels fastened in the center. The avalanche danger was low, but that didn't mean we could slack off. We'd follow the rules—carrying shovels and PIEPS and skiing close to the trees.

Lynne let me set the pace, seeing as how I was the lame one. The morning air was, as usual, lung freezing, but each labored breath warmed us as the sky started to lighten. We hadn't been hiking ten minutes, and already the old quads and calves were exploding, my heart thumping in Dolby through my ears and temples.

"How's it going?" Lynne asked.

"Sucking pond water," I wheezed back.

"Take it slow. We've got plenty of time."

"This not slow enough for you?" I was using my poles as ballast, sticking them into the existing indentations on the sides of the boot tracks.

"Just think about that beer we're going to pound after work."

"Yeah," I wheezed back.

"P.S., I've been seeing someone," Lynne said, perhaps to get my mind off being such a piker.

It worked. Stopping in my tracks, I turned to face her. "Guy or girl?"

"Guy." Lynne had been a lesbian all through college but had started giving heterosexuality a try since moving to the land of men.

"I know him?"

"I don't think so. His name's Max Wright? He's—"

"A doctor."

"How did you know?"

"ESP."

"Seriously, you know Max? He doesn't really hang out at the mountain much."

"He's my vag man."

"No shit," she said. "How is he? At that, I mean."

"Very thorough."

"I always wondered about his bedside manner. You know, when he's on the job."

"I thought he was great," I said, trying to pick up the pace somewhat.

"I'm still not sure what I think of him. I mean, he's *cute*."

"Yeah, a little too cute for a gyno if you ask me."

"And he's good in bed."

"Do I really want to hear about this?"

"Well, haven't you ever wondered about gynos? There they are, staring at coochies all day long . . . I used to wonder about it. Like, do they ever get turned on?"

"If you ever find out the answer to that question, please keep it to yourself."

"I already asked him."

"Tell me he said no."

"He said no." She used the same tone of voice you might use to discuss the laundry.

"You sound thrilled," I said.

"I don't know. He's cool and everything, I'm just not sure I'm into it," she said, hawking a loogie. "Women are just so much more complex."

"You mean psycho."

"Exactly."

"And you like that."

"What's love without a little adventure, I always say."

"I'm starting to think too much adventure in that department might not be a great thing."

"Well, you don't really need to worry about it anymore. You've got Jack, right?"

"Right," I said, even though it was my relationship with Jack I'd been referring to. It wasn't that I didn't love him, it was all the extenuating circumstances, wearing me out.

We huffed and puffed a while longer, removing hats and gloves, and undoing pit zips as we went. Getting into the zone, I tried to keep my breathing steady in the thin air. As I warmed up, I began to visualize the climb as a simple succession of steps, my only duty putting one foot in front of the other.

A gray mist hovered low in the valley, but it looked like it would probably clear off by noon. The tree coverage became more sporadic as we approached the top, fat magpies and potguts hopping in the snow among the pines.

"How you feeling?" Lynne asked.

"Not as bad as I thought I would."

"The thing about dating men is—" she said, picking up where we'd left off.

"So what, you're just *dating* now?"

"The thing about men is," she continued, "they're so cut and dry, you know what I mean? Maybe I need a little more drama in my life or something."

"What, like guys can't be drama queens?" I asked, thinking specifically about my college boyfriend Caleb. That guy had bigger identity problems than Anthony Perkins—jock as a freshman, prepster sophomore year, and finally, a long-haired, ripped-jeans-and-sandal-wearing Deadhead à la Bob Weir— when he dropped me for a muscular vegan with leg hair. "Believe me, you can find guys who will provide that."

"Maybe. But they're not quite as cute about it, you know?"

A golden retriever ran up the trail past us. "Hey, Loopy!" I called, causing her to wag her tail toward me and stick her nose in my crotch. Looking back, I saw Speed hoofing it, his uniski sticking up from his backpack, a red bandanna tied around his head. "How come I can't get away with that?" he asked, stopping briefly as Lynne and I moved aside to let him pass. When climbers are on a roll, it's best to get out of the way fast.

"Thankya, tele-mammas."

"Speed, Lynne, Lynne, Speed," I said. I saw by his expression, he didn't have time for chitchat.

Nodding at him, Lynne said, "Hey." She looked intrigued.

"Lynne, it's a pleasure," Speed said matter-of-factly as he moved past. "Don't eat too much bark on your way up!" he called back.

Pulling a Clif bar out of her pack and taking a couple of large, quick bites, Lynne asked, "Who was that?"

"Speed? He's our next-door neighbor."

"Where's he from?"

"Tennessee. Nice guy. A vet."

"That's cool," she said. "I like men who're into animals."

"No, a veteran, not veterinarian."

"Oh. *That's* different. Of what war?" she asked, the Clif bar bulging out her cheeks like those of a baseball player on the mound.

"Don't choke," I said. "Desert Storm. Special Ops."

"You *must* be joking."

"You did notice he only has one arm?"

Cocking her eyebrow, she smiled.

"You think he's cute?"

"Kinda. Here, eat some of this Rumpelstiltskin," she said, handing me the bar.

"Rumpelstiltskin?"

She shrugged. "Thought it sounded good. So what's the deal, did you and Jack make up?"

"Sort of," I said, sinking my teeth into the oaty chocolate. "These things are better than Powerbars, don't you think?"

"You want to tell me about it?"

"And ruin a perfectly good morning?"

"All right. Don't."

"He wants to move back and ride with a team down in Salt Lake this summer."

"And you want to stay here."

"Yeah."

"His wife lives down there, doesn't she?"

"Her, and a few other unsavory characters I'm not too thrilled about."

"Well, I don't want you to move back there, that's for damn sure." Lynne had been living in her parents' deluxe vacation home since graduating from Smith three years ago. I didn't hold the money against her though. She wasn't two-faced about it, and she was extremely generous. She ski-instructed for the sheer pleasure. I think that's what enabled her to enjoy herself on the job a little more than most.

"I just wish I had a clue," I said. "I'm not too thrilled about the idea of waiting tables for the rest of my life, you know?"

"I hearya."

"And then, not that I'm going to make it, but what if Pete Laurey decides to make me a star?" I said, batting my eyelashes coquettishly.

"I think what you meant was, what if Pete Laurey decides to make *me* a star," she said, taking the bar back from me and chomping into it. Lynne and I worked this faux competitive thing. Having said that, I couldn't say that I wouldn't be the tiniest bit POed if she made it and I didn't.

"Yeah, now that I think about it," she said, "maybe you *should* move down to Salt Lake. Why even bother trying out?"

"Look, I may not be at the top of my game today, but when Pete Laurey comes to town, you better watch your *ass*."

"Ooooh hooo *hooo*! You're *killin'* me," she said, hoisting her pack back on and forging up the hill ahead of me. "No more Mister Nice Guy."

Now it wasn't a question of feeling like it or not. I pushed it to stay on her tail, never more than a couple of boot lengths behind. By the time we reached the top, I felt as high and beat as I'd felt all season.

The warm smell of polyproed sweat wafted up from my snug-fitting Hot Chillys turtleneck as we sat on top of our jackets, Velcroing on kneepads, guzzling Exceed out of Nalgenes, and watching the sun move higher into the sky. Speed was nowhere in sight.

Finally Lynne stood up and said, "All right, yo*cheeze*. Time to free the heel."

Kneeling down on one knee, I lined the three pins in the front of my boot up with the three pins sticking up from the binding and secured the clamp.

"You really should consider looking into some new gear," she said, staring down at me.

"I'll get right on that, Paris," I said.

"Seriously, Betty, if it's a question of money—"

"It's always a question of money, Lynne. You know that," I said, giving her brand-new setup the once-over. "Those boots and bindings really make a difference?"

"Uh, yeah. They do. When did you say your birthday was again?"

"February."

"Perfect," she said, giving me a chipper look. "And now, if you'll excuse me, the time has come for you to eat my dust."

Jumping into the bowl, she executed several flawless turns. Lifting her heel, she brought her uphill knee down while thrusting the downhill ski forward, making the quasi-balletic hop-turns that are the signature of telemarking the steeps. The waxy bottoms of her skis made crisp shooshing noises on the cold, dry surface of the morning snow. She stopped, waiting for me to catch up. "Snow's pretty good," she said.

"A little cruddy, but there's plenty of it," I concurred.

"After you," she said, holding her pole out and bowing slightly.

"Don't mind if I do." I was cautious, turning often, keeping my speed in check, stomach rising and falling the way it might on a winding road with lots of unexpected twists and dips. There's nothing quite like linking turns together in the back-country at dawn. I kept it conservative though. I didn't want to injure myself on the first day out.

Lynne let things run a little more freely, humming down at an exhilarating pace that was fun to watch. The girl had it, no question. I was sure Pete Laurey would think so too.

There had been no significant snowfall in several days, so the fall line was slightly chewed with other tracks. On the bright side, the cold weather and lack of sun had kept the consistency reasonably light and easy to maneuver. That said, when you're out of shape, you're out of shape, and only a slow buildup back to strength can make you feel like a killer again. It didn't take a genius to figure out, the next couple of weeks were going to be a bitch.

chapter 16

Jack and I had been apart for all of three hours, and it felt like I was missing a limb. Sitting on one of the benches, using all the strength in my hands and biceps, I pulled the tongue of my Lange boot open as far as it would go and, pointing my toe, let the painful cramming session begin.

Back in the day, the salesmen at Hickory & Tweed in Armonk had sold me on a pair of slipperlike Nordica rear entries—quintessential bunny boots. I got rid of them shortly after moving out west because the boys gave me nothing but, as they liked to say, "scorn and ridicule." They sure were easier to put on than those high-performance Langes though. Just flip down the back and stick your foot in.

"Betty."

As soon as Jack and I locked eyes, it was like one of those

running-through-the-field-in-slow-motion love scenes. Like we hadn't seen each other in years.

We were demonstrating proper P.D.A. when over by his locker Dan coughed. "Get a room." He was in one of his muscle shirts, pulling on a pair of long johns.

"I *missed* you, Betty."

"I missed you too," I said.

"I *missed* you, I *missed* you," Dan whined. "Jeez, you two *do* live together, right? Just so you know, Betty? I didn't miss you." He punctuated his point with a fart and thumped his stomach like a bongo.

Jack said, "I've been thinking about it, and I'm really going to try and make it back here for Pete Laurey."

"What about Salt Lake?"

"Let's play it by ear, okay? Hey, do we have time for a tram before lineup?" Jack asked.

"I'm bushed," I said.

"I'll do a tram withya, Wacky Jacky," Dan said.

"Go ahead," I said. "I'm gonna head over to the Bear Claw and grab a cup of joe."

"Well then, I'm coming with you," Jack said.

The line for the tram was already snaking around the back of Nick Wilson's cafeteria, with tourons and local jokers alike. Jared and Monica, a couple of the Kids from next door, were standing on the end of it with their snowboards. Jared worked as a busboy at the Moose, and Monica was a housemaid at the new Four Seasons. They were eighteen, taking a year off before college. Jack and Jared gave each other the brother handshake.

"Dude," Jared said, nodding his head up and down. He looked very high. "Thanks for the sweet *ride* this morning."

"Yeah, that *oregano* you lent us for the *spaghetti sauce* was *amazing*," Monica said, her eyes drooping.

"No problem," Jack said.

"We'll hook you up with some tall boys later on," Jared said.

"Don't worry about it," Jack said.

As we continued our schlump toward the Bear Claw, Jack said, "They ran out." By way of explanation.

I wasn't sure how I felt about Jack being the Snoop Dogg of our enclave but reasoned, when I was their age . . . They probably thought he was pretty damn cool.

Lynne was sitting on one of the stools in the Bear Claw drinking a tall latte. "Howdy, pard," she said. "Hey, I forgot to mention, I've got some free passes to the gym at the Pines. You're welcome to them if you want to go in and do some of the classes. Might help get you back into shape."

"Are you calling me an ass-dragger?"

"Your tooshie's a bit smooshy, that's all," she said, smiling into her cup.

"That's very sweet of you," I said.

"Seriously. The spinning classes are pretty good, and I've been doing some yoga."

"I fucking hate yoga," I said, thinking a good dose of Ashtanga was probably *exactly* what I needed.

"Good for the stress," she said, raising her eyebrows, tilting her head.

"Oh, so now I'm *stressed*." She was absolutely right.

"Just a suggestion," she said.

The Pines is a pretty hoity-toity place. There was no way I could have afforded a membership there. It was a very nice offer. "I'm all over it," I said.

By nine-thirty, the sun was up and shining, the sky turning darker shades of blue. Hoss stared at his clipboard, his Ray-Ban Wayfarers pulled to the tip of his nose, a stogie sticking out the side of his mouth. Over his shoulder, I saw Charlene. *What was she still doing here?*

"Betty, I'm gonna welcomeya back with a private," Hoss said, motioning my subject forward. This here's Mr. Cecil Black."

Cecil Black wasn't paying attention. His eyes were glued to Charlene, who was sidling up to Jack.

"Hi, Cecil," I said, sticking my hand out, tilting my head into his line of vision.

"Oh, hey. Hi," he said, taking my hand.

He had on an expensive jumper, one crumpled cuff caught sloppily on the top of his rear-entry boot, a tiny pair of rental skis (given his enormous stature, he had to be six-four, six-five), and poles leaning precariously against his stomach.

"I'm Betty Winters."

He nodded. He looked slightly terrified and a little sad. "My girlfriend," he said, nodding over toward Charlene, who was by then heading toward the gondola alongside Jack sharing a good yuck, "insisted I take a lesson."

This was new. Usually it was the men who insisted their significant others take a lesson. I'd had one young woman the week I got sick who'd told me her boyfriend had given her an ultimatum—learn to parallel by the end of the week or no engagement ring.

It was as good an excuse for getting out of marriage as I'd ever heard. I gave her all I was worth, but she was hopeless. In the end, I figured I'd saved her in a way. Or maybe she'd saved herself. She was a sweet girl, and clearly, the guy was a dingbat.

Max Wright was standing over by Lynne all duded up in his North Face threads. If he skied as well as he doctored, my prognosis was he was quite the catch.

"This whole trip was really her idea. She came out a couple of weeks ago on a girls' trip and insisted I had to bring her back to see what the Jackson Hole experience was all about," Cecil Black said.

His skin was pretty pasty. A little more bran in his diet probably wouldn't have hurt.

"Wow," I said, with my trademark instructor's enthusiasm, "sounds like she really likes it here."

"She sure likes that instructor. What's his name—"

"Jack Catcher," I said. It was weird how Charlene didn't get me too riled. I could tell she wasn't Jack's type.

"Right. Jack. Good-looking guy."

"Hey," I said, chucking his elbow, "you're not exactly unattractive." It was true, he wasn't unattractive; he wasn't what you'd call a *looker* either. His mustache was sort of dweeby— a far cry from ski patrol manliness, and he had a slight paunch. Let's just say, he wasn't exactly a *specimen*. I wouldn't hold that against him though. I had a feeling Mr. Black had some greenbacks to spare, so I was going to do my darnedest to have him wedeling (a series of short, quick parallel turns, this technique is generally employed on groomers by hotdog wannabes) his flabby ass off by the end of the two hours.

"Well, Cecil," I said, taking his skis and locking them into the bindings, "first thing you want to make sure to do is keep your skis clamped together until you're ready to use them. Makes them easier to carry."

"Right," he said, embarrassed by his slovenliness.

"So, what kind of a skier are you?" I asked, knowing he was a beginner at best.

"Well, I sort of just started when Charlene and I got together a year ago. We were in Vail last Presidents' Day. I took a week of lessons there. I'm not sure," he said, shaking his head. "I guess I'm a beginner? High beginner, low intermediate?"

"Okay. Well then, why don't we start over on Eagle's Rest?"

"That's green, right?"

"Green all the way," I said, gung ho.

"Because I took a fall yesterday afternoon. I've got this pain in my shoulder," he said, bending up his elbow and rotating it. "It feels okay right now."

"Not to worry. We'll take it real easy, and see how you're feeling. How does that sound?"

For the first time since we'd been paired up, Cecil looked me in the eye, his face the picture of gratefulness and relief. "That sounds perfect."

When we'd finally gotten ourselves on the chair, I asked, "So, what do you do out in the real world?"

"Oh, I'm a computer geek," he said.

A Bill Gates *computer geek*? I wanted to ask but didn't.

Cecil said, "Charlene doesn't have much patience with me. That's why she's making me take a lesson. She's a much better skier than I am."

"Not after this morning she's not gonna be."

He smiled. He was loosening up. I felt kind of sorry for him. I bet Charlene could be a real pain in the ass.

"I like the mountains and everything. I'm happy to bring her on these vacations. Sometimes I just wish I could spend the day in the hot tub."

"I hearya," I said.

"Here's the thing," he said. "What I'd really like to do is move past the snowplow. You think I could learn to parallel? I'd *love* to be able to do that. Impress Charlene. She's such an expert."

I had my doubts about that last bit. "Hey, there's no shame in snowplowing," I said. "It's the foundation for everything that comes after."

He looked like a kid who'd just been told he couldn't have the toy of his heart's desire. This was no way to begin a lesson. You had to keep people's dreams alive. As we approached the top I said, "Why don't I see how you're doing and we'll take it from there?"

"I can live with that," he said.

His chair skills were adequate, no major freak shows there, but to go from a wedge turn to paralleling in two hours (despite my previous bravado) was not going to happen. I told Cecil to head on down. I'd follow right behind, see where he was at.

"The thing is," he said, turning to me before he got started, "I got pretty shaken up by that fall. I think I may have pulled something." His brow was knit, his entire face a study in tension. Fear One, Fear Two, the whole cavalcade stomped through him.

"Tell you what," I said. "Why don't you follow close behind me to start? Just keep your eyes up. We'll take it nice and slow, okay? I want you to remember to keep pressure on your downhill ski. We'll make a few big, long turns."

"Okay," he said, breathing out short and quick.

"All right, here we go now, eyes up!" I said as we began, my head in owllike posture, keeping him in view at all times.

Once he started moving, Cecil began looking a whole lot more confident. As though all he'd needed to do was convince himself he could do it. I had to say, his plowing skills were remarkably solid. I stopped after several turns and said, "You look great. You've got one of the best snowplows I've ever seen. I'm not kidding."

Did I detect a blush?

"Thanks," he said. "I'm not too fast but—"

"Let's take it one step at a time." The positive reinforcement was working its magic. The truth was, with Cecil, I meant it. He really wasn't half bad. I was a little blown away. "I think we should start focusing on the stem christie. You know what that is?"

"Is that like parallel?"

"It's what comes before. Here, watch me. You want to come across with your skis parallel, weight on the downhill ski, snowplow into your turn," I called, enunciating loud and slow during the demo, "bringing your skis back parallel as you come around. See if you can handle one of those!"

He stood for a moment collecting his thoughts, psyching himself up, and finally began to move, executing the stem christie exactly as I'd demonstrated. "Have you been lying to me, Cecil Black? You've done this before, haven't you?"

His face was all red again as he shook his head and gave a giddy laugh. "No, I swear, that was my first time," he said.

"*Man*, you're good. Let's see you do another one."

By the time we'd reached the bottom, I could officially say that Cecil Black was the quickest learner I'd ever had. He'd already begun linking his turns. The way he was going, paralleling by the end of the lesson might not be such a stretch after all.

After several flawless runs on Eagle's Rest, I asked Cecil if he thought he was ready to take it up to one of the intermediate runs on Après Vous.

"You think I can handle it?" he asked.

"I know you can," I said. "It's not much steeper and the runs are longer."

"Sounds good to me," he said.

Our lesson was coming to its grand finale. I knew that if he skied the intermediate run as flawlessly as he'd skied Eagle's Rest all morning, it would go a long way to getting rid of his greatest impediment, his low self-image.

It was nearing high noon, the sun warming us up so we could take off our hats. The snow had softened to that sweet, smooth consistency, making it easier to push around. On the

chair, Cecil closed his eyes and breathed in deeply. "Betty," he
said, "this has been one of the best mornings of my life."

"Oh go on," I said.

"I'm serious," he said, pushing his sunglasses up so I could
see his eyes.

"Well, thanks for saying so, Cecil, I appreciate it." In the
back of my mind, I hoped he'd express his sentiments monetarily. But the truth was, pupils like Cecil were rewarding in
their own right. In the course of two hours he'd gone from a
scared pudgeball with a dweeby mustache to a man in charge.
I'd gained a whole new respect for him. I knew from experience
that the kinds of breakthroughs he'd been having all morning
had probably brought him closer to God. Not to be sappy, or a
weird religion freak or anything, but skiing can elicit miracu-
lous transformations in a person.

The sunlight reflected off the snow, lending a warm spirit of
optimism to an otherwise cold and dreary winter. Cecil was
turning like a champ, and we weren't lollygagging either, we
moved right out, footloose and fancy free. "You are getting a
gold star for this," I said at a rest stop.

"I'm not half bad, am I?"

"You're a whole lot better than that!" For me, guys like Cecil
were what teaching was all about—helping people improve
their skills, gain more confidence.

We were at the apogee of our lesson, Cecil was feeling like
a superstar, and I was taking all the credit, when on the flats
toward the bottom, he crossed his tips and went down. His first
fall all lesson.

He'd been skiing slow, so I wasn't too concerned when I saw him lying there.

Not moving.

I thought he was pulling one of those "I'll just rest here a minute" maneuvers. It happens when you're embarrassed, so you pretend that you sort of *meant* to fall. Or conversely, you overplay the fall to show what a good sport you are.

Stopping up above, I asked, "You okay?" He didn't respond, so I got closer. "Hey, Cecil, talk to me."

Nothing.

Rapidly removing my skis, I bent down over him and placed my hand on his shoulder. No movement.

"Cecil?" I said, turning his face up from the snow, careful in case he had a neck injury.

His skin was even paler than it had been at the start of the lesson, his lips turning blue.

"Jesus fucking Christ." Wild-eyed, I looked around. "Hey!" I called to a young woman skiing by. "We need some help here. Ski down and tell them we've got an emergency!"

All right, get it together, Betty, this is no time to crack up. My heart was pumping like a jackhammer. I'd had first-aid training years ago, before getting my lifeguard certificate. Flashbacks of the fake rubbery dummy rushed into my head. I had to stay calm, be efficient.

Rolling Cecil over wasn't easy. He was a big guy, and I had to be careful not to hurt him. I checked for the pulse on his neck and couldn't feel one. He was unconscious. I opened his mouth, checked for obstructions, tilted his head back, pinched his nose, and began administering mouth-to-mouth. Putting my hands just below his chest plate, I pushed, counting to fifteen, gave him two more breaths, and started pushing again.

Holy Mother of God. I was trying to pump his heart for him, bring him back to life. *Please, please . . .* "Cecil! Wake up! Can you hear me? Wake up, Cecil Black!"

I don't know how many minutes went by before Bob was kneeling beside me. "Is he breathing?"

Cecil had resumed breathing several minutes earlier, but he was still only semiconscious.

"How long was he out for?" Bob asked, strapping an oxygen mask to his face.

"I'm not sure," I said. "Two minutes, three?"

"Let me in there," Bob said, taking over while the other patroller placed the gurney beside him and, working quickly, lifted him into the sled. "Follow us," Bob said.

chapter 17

Bob sat with his arm around me in the hospital waiting area. "It's not your fault, Betty, you did everything you could do. The guy was going to have a heart attack anyway."

Staring straight ahead, I nodded. *Maybe I'd pushed him too hard?* He'd been scared, more scared perhaps than he'd let on.

"In cases like these, you have to say to yourself, at least they were having fun, right? Hey, look at it this way, you saved the guy's life," Bob said.

We'd put out a search for Charlene, but she still hadn't made it to the hospital. She was probably getting her money's worth out of Jack. It was all too much.

The look on Cecil's face when he'd gotten his first parallel turn down . . . it was like he'd been *delivered*. It was like, for once in his pasty, branless life, Cecil Black felt *cool*. The poor guy. All he wanted to do was please *her*, and here he was, with a full-blown coronary. I wondered if Charlene would even care.

Two hours later, Jack and Charlene showed up looking as though they'd benefited from a day in the sun. They had apparently been skiing over at the quad and missed all of the notes on the board by the lift. "Betty," Jack said, intuiting all was not well, "what's going on?"

"Did he blow his knee out again?" Charlene asked, pulling her fuzzy blue ear warmer off and shaking out her hair.

Bob stepped in and led her to a corner of the tiny waiting area, speaking softly so no one else could hear.

"Jack, where were you?"

"We grabbed some lunch over at the Alpenhof."

"Wait, they told me you were over on the quad," I said, confused.

"We were, but then Charlene got hungry and offered to buy me lunch."

I smelled the beer and onions on his breath.

"Take it easy, Betty, we just grabbed a couple of burgers."

"What? What are you telling me? Where is he?" Charlene sounded bitchier than I would have expected. "I don't believe this!" she said, smacking her hand on her forehead like "I coulda had a V8!"

It was hard to tell what she was going through. She was neither crying nor particularly hysterical. She might have been in shock.

Walking slowly over to Jack and me with an incredulous look on her face, she said, "I have had that man on a strict diet for *weeks*. And does he lose any weight? I swear, he must have been sneaking peanut brittle behind my back."

Cecil Black was in stable condition three days later when I went to the hospital for my daily visit. I was sitting next to his bed as he dozed when a trim redhead, neatly accessorized, came into the room. She did not look pleased to see me. "Who the *hell* are you?" she asked.

I stood and said, "I'm Betty Winters. I was giving him a lesson when it happened."

"Oh," she said, looking somewhat relieved. "They told me about you. Said if you hadn't administered CPR when you did—" She broke off, tears gathering in her eyes.

I was on the verge of saying something stupid like "And you are?" But she saved me by sticking out her hand. "I'm Karen Black, Cecil's wife."

Cecil, you sly dog. I guess you never can tell. I mean a guy like Cecil. He must have been *really* loaded. I wondered how much she knew. About Charlene that is.

"I understand he was here with someone?" she said, breathing in primly.

"I wouldn't know about that," I said. It didn't seem right to narc on Cecil, or upset her.

"Betty?" she said, all business now, "please don't bullshit me."

I could feel my eyelid beginning to twitch. Man, was I a lousy liar. "Mrs. Black," I said, "I knew your husband, I mean, I've *known* your husband for all of the two hours I spent giving him a ski lesson."

"And you didn't notice if he was *with* anyone?"

"No," I said, "I didn't."

Turning away from me, she went over and sat in the chair I'd just vacated and began whispering to Cecil. I had no idea where Charlene was. I just thanked God she wasn't here.

Out in the waiting area, I caught Max Wright out of the corner of my eye. "Betty," he said, taking the seat next to mine. "Cecil Black. Talk to me."

"He was a student of mine. He had a heart attack," I said, noticing how spiffy he looked in his scrubs.

He shook his head. "That is some bad luck."

There was something so open and inviting about his face, it made me want to confide in him. "Yeah," I said. "His wife just showed up. I'm just glad his girlfriend wasn't here."

"That bitchy blond woman I've been seeing around isn't his wife?"

I shook my head.

"What a slimeball," he said.

"Pretty strong words for a guy who just skirted death," I said, feeling suddenly defensive. Whether of Cecil Black or myself, I didn't know.

"Hey, *I'm* still alive and kicking," he said.

Touchy.

"I'm sorry," he said. "I guess I just don't have a lot of sympathy for guys who cheat on their wives. Or the other way around for that matter."

Sounded like he was speaking from experience. I'd been ra-
tionalizing Jack and me for a long time, but it wasn't like I
couldn't appreciate the truth when I heard it. I mean, you can
get away with some pretty ugly stuff with that whole live-every-
day-like-it's-your-last attitude. Because *plenty* of shit flies under
that umbrella—the good, the bad, and the ugly. Sometimes I
wasn't completely convinced I would have been as in love with
Jack if the whole situation hadn't been so breathtakingly dramatic and doomed in a way.

The conversation was bringing me down so I asked, "What
brings you here?"

"Delivery."

"I didn't know you were an ob-gyn," I said.

"Yup," he said. "By the way, how did everything go with the
Diflucan?"

"Very well, thanks." It felt strange to be discussing my
vagina with him. Indirectly of course.

"And the flu?"

"All gone."

"You certainly look better," he said, giving me that smile.

"Has anyone ever told you, you look like Jake Gyllenhaal?"

"Yeah, actually. One of the nurses. I don't even know who
the guy is, I just hope he's not too funny looking."

"Not *too* funny looking," I said, realizing I was flirting.

"Right," he said, going along. "I'll take it as a compliment
then. So what's going on with all of this Cecil Black business?"

"I'm not really supposed to talk about it. The Corporation's
got its lawyers on the case—"

"Say no more," he said, holding up a hand.

"By the way, Lynne mentioned you guys were seeing each other?"

"Did she?" he asked, giving away nothing.

I could tell he didn't want to talk about it, so I said, "She's a cool chick," and let it drop. "And another thing, I still haven't gotten a bill for your services."

"Don't hold your breath," he said, standing up.

I wondered if Lynne had told him I was some lame-ass kid who couldn't afford to see a doctor. Or maybe she'd paid him back in kind? Truth was, if Jack's father hadn't helped out, we'd have been putting groceries on the credit card again.

"Hey, how about I make you guys dinner one of these nights?" I asked.

"That would be lovely," he said, sort of tongue-in-cheek.

"How about Thursday next week?"

"I'll check my calendar," he said, raising his eyes to the ceiling like he was calculating it in his head. "I'm free," he said.

I waited for him to say something about Lynne, but he didn't. So I said, "I'll give Lynne a call and see if she can make it."

"Good deal," he said.

Dolores, an attractive woman in bike shorts and an athletic bra, walked into the small, dimly lit room carrying a pair of cycling shoes. She had kinky, medium-length hair, pulled up into a tight ponytail. The muscle tone in her legs and arms was hard to argue with.

"Anyone's first time?" she asked, looking around the room. Lynne was already pedaling calmly, her racing shoes clipped in. My biking shoes were a pair of hand-me-downs from Jack, with stiff soles, no clips. I cinched them into the baskets and raised my hand.

"You ride?" she asked.

"Road and mountain bikes," I said. Jack had gotten me into biking when I'd helped him train the previous season. By bungeeing the handlebars of my bike to the seat of his, I could

stick with him while he more or less pulled me up the mountains.

Checking out the adjustments I'd made on the stationary
bike, she said, "Looks good. You might be able to bring the
seat back a little. Make sure your shoes are strapped in good
and tight. You have water?"

"You can share mine." Lynne had a gigantic water bottle
resting in her holder.

Clicking in the tape, Dolores put on a headset, bringing the
mike to her lips. "Okay, we'll be doing four major climbs during the forty-five minutes, but I want everyone to be good and
warm first."

*Midnight, it's raining outside, he must be soaking wet, everyone is
sleeping tight . . .*

"Now relax your left leg, pedaling only with the right. And
switch! Turn up your resistance one full revolution . . ."

By the time we got to Bronski Beat's "Why?," small pools of
sweat were glistening on the floor beneath my bike. Lynne was
in the zone while I tried to maintain pedal speed by keeping the
resistance lower than it should have been.

"Now third position and up!"

There was no way to get comfortably into the half seat without cranking up the resistance. As I fumbled with the knob,
Dolores got off her bike, came toward me, and turned it up to
where I had to put my entire body into it, pulling up *and* pushing
down on the pedals, rocking from side to side . . . *That smarts.*

*We're gonna lay around the shanty, momma, and put a good buzz
on . . .*

"Come on, people—*ride!* I want you to see the top. Push it! Don't stop till you drop!"

When it was all over, my endorphins had come full circle—kicked in, rallied, and putzed—several times. My legs were noodles. If I did this every other day for the next ten, my quads would thank me.

Sunday afternoon the Stagecoach was packed. The decibels had gone up considerably over the last half hour or so as people came in from the mountain. Every skid and his brother was hanging out, drinking fifty-cent Coors out of plastic cups, playing foosball, and taking the odd turn on the dance floor.

The Stagecoach band was in good form that night. Curly Marks sat in on some of the classics. A Robert Plant look-alike, Curly was a serious rock and roller with long, out-of-control hair and tight, ankle-hugging jeans. A definite standout in the Gore-Tex crowd. I don't even think he skied. He had a great voice, and a cool three-pack-a-day habit. He belted out the Prince tune "I Could Never Take the Place of Your Man" as Jack and I sat in the back by the snack bar eating Stagecoach burgers. "You want to dance?" I asked.

"You go ahead," he said, taking a sip of his beer. He wasn't in a great mood about having to leave for Salt Lake the next day. At least, he was pretending not to be. Convincing some retard at the INS that he and Muriel were still married and had never been more in love would be a rough sell no matter how you sliced it.

I guess I felt pretty secure about Jack's feelings, because if I had to sum up my attitude toward those two, *have at it* pretty much did the job. They were married, who was I to start throwing threats around? The odd thing was, I wasn't sure I minded if the two of them *did* get together for old times' sake. It *had* presumably happened before.

On top of Cecil Black and Pete Laurey, the situation was tense at best. I really just wanted to check out for a while. "No, it's okay," I said, taking another gulp of beer, rocking my head to the beat.

"Seriously, Betty, go on up there. I don't mind." Jack wasn't really much of a dancer. I mean, he knew his way around a mosh pit, but he was no Grandmaster Flash.

"No. I want to stay here with you," I said unconvincingly, dragging a fry through the piles of ketchup, mayo, and mustard on the wax paper of my burger basket and sticking it in my mouth. The fries were the thick, soggy kind I'm not too crazy about, but I was on a mission to pack on a few more pounds before tryouts. There really is no such thing as an emaciated ass kicker.

"You want another beer?" Jack asked.

"Sure," I said. It was one of those late afternoons that make you feel like dying. Except we'd had a decent day on the mountain and neither of us was working that night, so it wasn't quite as bad. It felt sort of good to be listening to Curly belt it out, survey the locals, put a little beer buzz on, and forget about life for a while.

You don't often see crackers getting down to the beat the way Speed was. Taller than most of the crowd, the guy was a wild man, totally uninhibited, twirling around, thrusting his

hips, a cigarette dangling from the side of his mouth. He em-
bodied that saying "Out here the odds are good, but the goods
are odd." For a one-armed vet, I had to admit, he looked pretty
sexy.

Spotting me in the back, he waved me over. Curly was giving
James Brown a run for his money with his own version of "I Feel
Good."

Fuck it, I thought. I wanted to feel good. Pressing through
the crowd, I had to say "excuse me" and "pardon me" about a
million times while keeping Speed in focus. Those skids moved
right out of the way too. They could be pretty polite.

"Hey, Sista Sledge!" Speed called, grabbing my hand and
hurling me into a frenzied two-step. People cleared the way as
he led me over, under, twirling, dipping. It was Fred Astaire and
Ginger Rogers all the way.

"Ba-ring it!" he shouted, looking happier than a muskrat at
a pie-eating contest. Or something. You know what I mean.

"Who knew?" I called.

"Oh, I gotcha, don't you worry," he said, as he thrust me
back, my head nearly touching the floor. "Now come to Papa,"
he said, hoisting me up. He reminded me of Hillsy, this guy I
knew at prep school who was famous for dancing the panties
off just about every debutante on the Social Register.

During an especially dizzying twirl, I saw Lynne and Max walk
in, pull off their hats, check out the scene. I watched Lynne
watch Speed. He just might have been what she'd meant by
"dramatic."

*　*　*

That night Jack and I didn't have sex. You would have thought, given the circumstances . . . I mean we weren't going to see each other for a couple of days and we hadn't ever been apart for longer than a couple of hours over the past six months. It felt like we *should* have wanted to.

Instead, we crashed early. I was going to ski up the service road in the morning before the lifts opened and get first tracks with Bob. I'd managed to bring myself back from the dead somewhat. It was a good thing too, because Pete Laurey would be in town the day after tomorrow.

chapter 19

Sitting alone at the kitchen table eating leftover spaghetti Bolognese and drinking orange juice, I stared up at the cupboard where the Classico jars were and wondered if it might not be a good time to spark one up. Jack was still in Salt Lake. Apparently, things had gotten complicated with the INS, *surprise, surprise.*

It was still early, six or seven o'clock. I rolled a joint, took it into the main room, and sat on the bed. *Atlas Shrugged* sat dog-eared on the bedside table next to the .357. Lighting the joint, I took the gun out of its holster, laid it on my lap, and cracked open the book. Sometimes when Jack wasn't around, the old paranoia really got the best of me. As the wind pushed against the plastic on the windows, my eyes went over the words, but all I could see were toothless inbreds busting through the front door. I was doing that thing again where you get to the bottom of the paragraph and realize you have no idea what you've just read. I was too wound up. Even *with* the pot. Back into the kitchen for an ashtray. The keys to the Subaru were in my pocket, Sorels ready and waiting by the door. I don't know. I guess I just felt like seeing some fresh faces.

Steve Packman, a.k.a. Pack, the old manager from the Moose, had opened up a bar and restaurant called Horse Creek just up the road that boasted "The Teton Mystery!"

I never did find out what it was. Or if I did, I can't remember anymore—petroglyphs? Some kind of magnetic force field?

"Betty getcher gun!" Pack called when he saw me come in. It's what he said every time he saw me. He was polishing glasses behind the bar. "Can I get forya?" The place was empty except for a couple of cowboys down at the end of the bar.

"Shot of Cuervo and a Bass back," I said.

"The lady wants to pardee," he said, popping the top off the Bass and holding up a frosty glass. "I forget, you take it straight from the bottle?"

"Usually," I said, "but that glass looks good."

Filling it halfway, he took the shot dispenser off the top of the Cuervo in order to give me a little extra. "What's cookin', darlin'?" Short and handsome, Pack was a competitive snow-mobiler in his spare time. We'd worked together at the Moose over the summer, before Jack had come to town. He had on the usual, Wranglers, cowboy boots, and a cowboy shirt. "Haven't seenya in a while. Been working?"

"Working and working out," I said.

"Doin' some twelve-ounce curls, haveya? Want some lime and salt with that?"

"No thanks," I said, throwing back the shot, shaking my head.

Checking his watch, he said, "Looks like it's tequila-thirty," and poured out two more shots. "I gotta have the lime at least," he said. We clinked glasses and threw them back in unison, then slammed them back on the bar. Grimacing, he said, "Ándale, ándale."

"*Arriba, arriba*," I responded.

Then, "Seen Jack around some."

"Is that right?"

"He comes in every once in a while," Pack said, leaning back against the register.

Some people call me the space cowboy . . .

"Some call me the gangster of luuuuv," Pack rejoined. "Now what the hell is he sayin'? I can never figure it out."

"Don't look at me," I said, my gut clenching into a ball. What the hell was Jack doing hanging out at Horse Creek?

"Lester!" Pack called to one of the cowboys at the end of the bar. "You know what that line is?"

"What, 'pompetus of love'?" Lester asked, tipping up his hat with a gnarled finger. "Not a clue."

"Damn. I gotta figure that out," Pack said, wiping the bar with a towel. "You good?" he asked.

"When was Jack in here?" I asked.

"I don't want any trouble," he said, holding up his hands.

"Then you better start talking," I said, sounding nastier than I meant to.

"No big deal. I seen 'im in here with some of his buddies from the mountain."

"What *buddies* from the mountain?"

"I don't know their names," he said, backpedaling. He picked up a clean glass and started polishing it.

I stared at my beer. Jack hadn't mentioned it. And why not? "Any women?" I asked.

"Now come on, Betty darlin'. You know I ain't a sneak."

"You're sounding pretty damn sneaky to me."

Holding his hands up in protest, he said, "Look. Don't start jumpin' to conclusions. Like I said, no big deal."

"*What's* no big deal?" I was steamed. The tequila hadn't just gone to my head, it was dancing up there like a can of Mexican jumping beans.

"All right, darlin', you know where my allegiances lie. . . . He was in here with some blond lady a couple of times. They looked like they were just friends. Relatives even."

"Kissing cousins or *what?*" I practically screamed.

"Now you see there, that's"—he shook his finger, searching for the word—"conclusions. I would like to buy you another shot," he said, turning and reaching for the Cuervo.

I'd never thought I was the jealous type before, but I suddenly felt sick with anxiety and rage. How had I managed to kid myself that Jack's behavior—his leaving Muriel for me—was strictly one isolated incident, a necessary action taken by a man hopelessly in love?

What goes around comes around . . . I grabbed my coat and headed for the door.

"You scared her off, Pack!" Lester called. "Come on, honey, that bastard don't know howda treat a lady."

I managed to look back and crack a flirtatious smile. You had to handle these cowboys right, make 'em think you were flattered.

"Come on now, Betty, it wasn't anything," Pack called.

"It's not your fault," I said, pushing my butt against the door.

Indeed. Who did I think I was anyway? Mata *Hari*? Did I think I was so *fine* I could turn a cheater around? Make a monogamist out of him? I didn't blame Jack. For him it was congenital. I blamed myself for being such a stupid, starry-eyed sucker.

"All right, people! Here's what I want you to do!"

Pete Laurey was at the bottom of Corbet's Couloir, a pair of Oakleys wrapped around his face, a bullhorn stuck to his mouth. Dan, Lynne, Speed, and I stood just back from the cornice, the tips of our various modes of transport reaching over the edge. The cornice hung so far out over the landing, it was impossible to see anything but Pete Laurey, ant-sized, standing down at the bottom, where the trail ran out.

"Begyer pardon?" Speed drawled, in a low, sassy voice.

It was a good thing the weather had cooperated; if there'd been any wind whatsoever, we really *wouldn't* have been able to hear Pete Laurey from down there. It wasn't the first time he'd explained things. He'd held a meeting in the hut at the top of the tram that morning, describing what he wanted us to do. What it boiled down to was "Tear it up."

We'd already jammed down the bumps on Thunder, peeled through the powder under the Headwall, and ripped through the crud on the Cirque. After each pitch, several people had been eliminated, so that we were now down to a crowd of about fifteen bums.

My motto has always been quit as soon as you start feeling tired, because that's when accidents happen. I was ashamed to admit, after all that jogging, climbing, skiing, spinning, stepping, lifting, and even *yoga* for Christ's sake, this bum was getting tired.

A camera guy, crouched at the edge of the cornice, poised to film takeoffs. Another was posted off to the side of the chute somewhere to catch close-ups of our landings, and a third was down at the bottom standing next to Pete Laurey. Mac was at the top, acting as organizer. Onlookers had skied around and stopped at the bottom to watch. Behind us were the remaining skiers, each champing at the bit to impress the king of the extreme video world.

He spoke loud and slow. "When I say *go*, I want you to come on down, one by one! Like I said, the more air you catch, the hotter your moves, the better chance you're going to have. Impress me!"

He was talking to some of the best skiers in the world, and let me tell you, I give myself credit for having the cojones to even lump myself in with that crowd. They were *mega*. Take a ride up just about any lift on that hill and you're likely to see not one but several world-class shredders. Jackson was crawling with them.

"I don't want anyone to have to be medevaced out of here, understand?" Mac said.

Lynne nervously tapped her skis one by one.

"I'm ready to get this party started," Dan said, staring out into the distance.

They'd closed off Corbet's three days previous to keep it from getting diced up by yahoos. Saying you'd done it no longer brought the *oohs* and *aahs* it once had. Pretty much any knucklehead could jump in there. It was how you looked when you did it that counted.

What made Corbet's slightly daunting from my point of view was that, unlike on all of the other shots we'd skied, catching air was a prerequisite. You couldn't get in there without your skis leaving the ground for an appreciable period of time. Moreover, any given launching spot off the cornice brought with it a greater or lesser degree of air. So in this instance, *where* you decided to launch from was as important as the quality of the launch itself.

"Anyone know what the landing was like three days ago?" Mac asked the crowd.

"Shit *yeah*," a boarder named Mudslide, with thick, peroxided hair, said. "It was *awesome.*"

"Care to share a few specifics there, Mudslide?" Mac asked.

"Not really," he said.

It was hard to say whether he couldn't give specifics because of his scanty hold on the English language or he just didn't want to share the info.

"I skied the bitch last week, pardon my French, darlin'," Speed said, giving a conciliatory nod to Lynne.

"And?" Mac asked.

"It was good, soft, plenty of snow, no problem. It'll probably be even better today. We've gotten what, another foot or so in there? It's gonna feel like jumpin' into a fine feather bed."

He and Lynne exchanged a look.

"Oh man," I said, shaking my head at her. "I don't even want to *know*."

Jack had called from Salt Lake early that morning to tell me he wasn't going to make it. When I asked him how things were over at Gibby's, he said that, actually, he'd decided not to stay with Gibby but on Muriel's couch. It looked better that way for the authorities.

I wondered whether he hadn't planned it that way all along. The fact that he told me about it kept it out of the realm of sneaking. And now wasn't the time to go off half-cocked over-thinking things. He'd laughed when I mentioned hearing about him hanging out at Horse Creek with "some blonde." Said that, sure, he'd stopped by there with Charlene a couple of times because she wanted to see what the local scene was all about, but that was it. "Come on, Betty," he'd said. "*Charlene?*"

More disturbing was the sheer, unadulterated fact that he'd pretty much made up his mind insofar as the summer was concerned. He wouldn't be going to South America no matter how you sliced it.

As for me, I wasn't feeling as strong as I could have maybe, as I stood there with my tips hanging off the cornice of Corbet's. But I *did* have a shot, perhaps not a big one but a shot nonetheless. And if I had a snowball's chance of making something of myself, by God, I was going to take it. Or else . . . or else the *Buckeye buffet!*

"All right, Speed, since you so gallantly shared your wisdom with the rest of us, I'm going to give you first dibs in there," Mac said.

"Aaaw, that's cold," Mudslide said.

"Either I'm next," Dan said, "or no more cunnilingus for you, my little friend."

Mac's face turned red. "Betty? Why don't you jump in after Speed, Lynne and Dan to follow."

"I can't get no respect," Dan said, tightening the Velcro on his gloves, zipping his shell up to his chin, and lowering his goggles.

"Kill it, Rodney," Mac said.

Everyone was quiet then, the only sound the screeching of a hawk circling overhead. My stomach was doing proverbial cartwheels. As I've already said, I wasn't crazy about catching air to begin with, especially when you couldn't see the landing. And here I was going to have to seek out the point at which to maximize the amount of air I was going to catch. Fear One, Fear Two, and a new brand of fear—fear of the unknown—began to overwhelm me. Not the ideal attack-the-hill mind-set needed for dazzling the glitterati. What was the worst that could happen?

"Go!" came Pete Laurey's tinned voice.

"Hasta la vista, babies," Speed said before jumping up higher than I thought possible for any human, never mind one with one arm and no poles, from a complete standstill. Once he was over the cornice, that was it, he was out of sight until he appeared again at the bottom of the chute.

Silencing the scary voices in my head, it was time to practice what I preached.

Lynne said, "Nail it, sister," just before Pete Laurey called "Go!"

Twenty feet back from the cornice, I stared toward the point where the overhang was widest. Pushing off, I skated toward it, prepared to fly.

It was the last thing I remembered before lifting my face out of a pool of blood in the snow. As I shook the cobwebs from my head, drops of red splattered against the white backdrop. One arm was forward, the other against my side. I was sprawled headfirst down the mountain, legs penguined, skis attached. "It looks like her nose," Pete Laurey said, leaning over me with one of the camera guys.

"You all right?" the camera guy asked.

A sharp pain shot up from my wrist. I couldn't speak.

"Might be broken," Pete said. "Which one is she?"

"That's"—pause—"Betty Winters."

"You alive?" Having returned my nose to the cool relief of the snow, I couldn't see any of them, but I did recognize Bob's voice. "Where does it hurt?" he asked.

"My wrist," I muffled.

"Anywhere else? How about your nose?"

"No, the wrist, just the wrist," I replied in that panicky, monosyllabic way people do when they're in serious pain but can't seem to get their point across.

"All right, Jorgy and I are gonna turn you over."

It was calming to have them in control.

"Christ, you look like Rocky Balboa," Jorgy said. "Sure that *nose* doesn't hurt?"

"It's my *wrist*!" I screamed, unable to stand it anymore.

"Looks like she's gonna need a ride," Bob said. "Sit tight, Betty, we'll have you down to the clinic in no time."

It was a good thing I was in so much pain, otherwise I know I would have been overcome with embarrassment. Any time you saw patrollers skiing someone down in one of those sleds, you couldn't help but feel slightly superior to the poor sucker bundled up inside. Now I was the poor sucker, and I wasn't too quiet about it either. As Bob and Jorgy steered me down, I began moaning uncontrollably.

The doctor at the mountain clinic was Austrian. He took one look at my face and, like everyone else, assumed I'd broken my nose, which he pressed and poked a couple of times. It was bloody but intact. Then he pulled off my glove, stared at my wrist a moment, and asked, "Where does it hurt?"

There are only so many places on a wrist you can injure. The whole thing felt pretty damn fucked to me. I didn't really even want to look at it, but when I did, I could see a white lump sticking up from the top, as if that little knob joint had rotated up from the side. "There." I pointed.

"Ah, *so*," he said.

Was this guy a comedian or what? He looked old enough to be a doctor, perhaps a bit too tanned . . .

Next thing I knew, the nurse was coming toward me with the

biggest-ass needle I'd ever seen. She rolled me over like a sack of potatoes and wrestled my bibs down. She was being so rough about it that, when she finally had my ass exposed, I thought she might spank me. Instead, she stuck me with the needle.

I watched the doctor nod to her then, and without their exchanging a word, she grabbed my elbow, he grabbed my hand, and they pulled in opposite directions, producing what had to be the acutest instance of agony I'm ever likely to experience. They did it so fast, I'm not even sure I had time to scream. It's all a bit cloudy now, because as soon as things were set, the morphine kicked in and everything was hunky-dory. Peachy keen. I'd never felt so good in my life.

Bob stood by as I chatted pleasantly with the nurse about how nice the warm plaster felt as she applied it. By the time she'd finished, my wrist was cocked inward at almost a right angle and the cast reached up to my armpit.

In the next cot over, a guy from Texas was getting his leg plastered. "Whatchoo in here for?" he asked, a happy morphine glow on his face. "Oh, I see nah. *Dayam.* That's one hell of a cast you got there. Where you from?"

"I live here," I said.

"Well all *right!*" he said, nodding and grinning like Goofy.

"I'm from the New York area originally."

"I'm not sayin' *nothin'* to that," he said.

"You?"

"Houston. Ever been?"

"Never been to Texas."

"Whoo, girl, you gotta visit. Best state in the Union."

"I've heard good things about Austin."

"Austin's nice."

It was like we were hanging out at the Moose waiting for someone to bring us a couple of drinks.

"What did you do to your leg there?"

"Shoot, I went down right under Casper, dumbest thing you ever saw. Blew out ma knee."

"Hey!" Lynne and Speed came in. "Holy moly, would you look at that," Lynne said.

"Welcome to the club," Speed added.

"Doesn't look too promising, does it?" I said, staring down at the hardening plaster like it was someone else's arm.

"Shee-it," Speed said. "What was it? A compound?"

"Something like that."

"Can one of you give her a lift home?" Bob asked.

"Yeah," Speed and Lynne said together.

"Have they called your parents?" Lynne asked.

"I'll call them later," I said.

"What about Jack?"

"I don't have the number there."

"The number where?"

"His wife's." It sounded so funny coming out, I started laughing. Morphine. I could see how people got addicted to that stuff. I knew once it wore off, I'd be in a world of pain.

"It's settled," Mom said. "I'm wiring you money, and you are taking the next plane out of there."

I'd waited a few days before giving Mom the news. I'd only called as a courtesy, to let her know what was going on, as any good daughter would. "I'm not coming home," I said.

"Listen to me, Elizabeth, I can take care of you here. You'll have nice food, your old room back, we'll go shopping . . ."

I'm not going to say I wasn't tempted. Even though she was making it all sound better than it would be, part of me wanted to be taken care of, revert to baby mode. I had to stay strong though. "Jack can take care of me," I said, not wanting to let on what a mess things were. It was almost like I didn't want her to know she'd been right. I hadn't quite admitted it to myself yet.

"How will you earn a living?"

"I'll figure something out."

"With a cast up to your armpit? Are you going to join the circus?"

"Look, Mom, I don't know," I said. Who was I kidding? I had a hundred bucks to my name, which would take care of gas and food for what—a week? Two? She was right, working with that bum arm would be next to impossible. Things with Jack were who knew what . . .

"Oh, don't be such a martyr. By the way, can we assume no news is good news?" she asked.

"I'm sorry, what news are we talking about?"

"You know, the *flu*."

That whole episode felt like years ago to me now. "It looks like I'm going to live," I said, not at all sure that was cause for celebration.

The next call I had to make was to Max Wright. Dinner would have to be canceled. Lynne had understandably passed, Jack was still down in Salt Lake doing what, or whom, I didn't know. Having blown my shot at stardom in the most spectacular way, I was crushed right back down to where I'd been two weeks earlier. It was four o'clock, the sinking hour, and I was feeling true to form.

"Doctor Wright's office," a woman answered.

"Hi, this is Betty Winters calling for Dr. Wright?"

"Regarding?"

"It's a personal call."

"Please hold."

The pay phone clicked. I stuck another quarter in. Jim

peered out of the office and called, "Come over and use our phone!"

I waved. "It's okay, I'm on hold."

I stayed on hold for another five minutes and was down to my last quarter when Max Wright finally got on the line. "Betty! I'll be down in an hour." He sounded hurried and slightly amped.

"Um, hey, yeah, that's why I'm calling."

"Look, you don't need to feel weird about the whole Lynne thing. It's no big deal. I still wouldn't mind coming down for a home-cooked meal, meet the ball and chain."

"Right. The thing is—"

"Yeah, tell her I'll be in in a minute," he said to someone in the background. "Sorry about that. You were saying?"

"Jack's not around and I broke my wrist, so it doesn't look like I'll be doing much cooking."

Or having much of a life in general.

"Oh, Betty. I'm sorry to hear that."

He really did sound sorry too.

"Hey, you've still gotta eat, right? I love that place down by you, Trail Creek? How about I come down, take you out for a meal?"

My eyes welled up. I'd been feeling like such crap, a kind gesture was all it took to get me choked up. "It's okay, you don't have to come all the way down here."

"Don't be ridiculous. I'm *comin'* down there, and you can't stop me. We'll order up a couple of martinis and some chicken-fried steaks. It's their specialty."

It had been a long time since anyone had taken me out for

dinner. And he sounded so upbeat. I decided it might be just what the doctor ordered. Pun intended. "You sure?"

"I'll see you in an hour."

My personal hygiene over the past few days had consisted solely of little bird baths in the sink. It was time to get out a plastic Albertson's bag and some rubber bands. Holding my arm out as best as I could from the acupuncture shower spray, I gripped the soap with my left hand like a man overboard gripping a life ring. I'm a righty, and let me tell you, I might as well not have had a left hand altogether for all the good it did me. Getting it to move in a lather-producing motion was almost more than I could handle.

And how was I going to be able to pour the shampoo out of that industrial-sized bottle of Pantene? Bending down, I picked it up, snapped the top with my thumb, squeezed a blob onto the shower floor, and quickly scooped it up. Patting it on my head, I thought of that test of coordination, what is it? Patting your stomach, swirling your head? Or swirling your stomach, patting your head? I patted and swirled, giving it my full concentration, twisting my long hair into knots under the lame spray.

I don't know how long I'd been in there, but I'd just gotten to soaping my ears when I heard the door boom open. "Betty? You here?"

"I'm in the shower!" I called.

Footsteps approached. "Betty?"

Turning off the spray, I called out again, "Here! In the shower!"

"Right! Sorry!" Max said.

"Why don't you grab yourself a beer!"

"Ten-four!"

Ripping the bag off my arm, I managed to get a towel around myself, holding it up under the cast. Tiptoeing out into the main room, I spotted Max over on the couch, Old Style in hand, thumbing through *Atlas Shrugged*.

"Excuse my—"

"Nothing I haven't seen before," he said, without looking up.

It stopped me up a little. I didn't know if he meant me, *specifically*, or he was just saying—in general like.

"What do you think of Ayn Rand?" he asked.

"Pretty good," I said, fumbling through Jack's flannels on the rack. "Makes me want to earn some money."

"What's the deal with the gun on the bedside table?"

That gun was a real conversation piece. "Jack likes to keep it there. For protection."

"What is it? Three fifty-seven?"

"Good guess."

"I've got one just like it. I keep it under lock and key, though."

The shape of the cast made it difficult to wear just about everything. One thing was certain, I wasn't going to be able to get a shirt over that arm without dropping the towel. I began to sweat. I swear, I didn't know how Speed got along. Okay, collect underwear, pants, shirt, go back into the bathroom, put them on.

"You need some help over there?" he asked.

"No, it's okay. I got it." If Jack were there, I probably wouldn't have been so stoic. It's weird how you show different faces to different people. Not that Max Wright hadn't seen me at my very worst . . .

I grabbed one of the flannels with such force that the hanger went flying.

"It's all fun and games," Max said, peering over his glasses.

"I'll be right back."

It must have taken me a good twenty minutes to get everything on. As for zipping and buttoning those Levi's—well, I got the zipper up at least. My long, wavy hair looked like a Brillo pad run amuck. How would I get a comb through that mess without ripping it out by the roots?

"No problem," Max said. He was very gentle about it too. Held sections to comb out the tangles without me feeling it. As for makeup, I rarely wore it. I probably would have put on a little concealer and blush or something for going out to dinner. I wasn't a total heathen. But I really didn't want him thinking I was trying too hard. Plus, it was too much of a pain in the ass anyway. A little moisturizer and I'd be good to go.

A spiffy new BMW X5 sat in the space that Jack's truck usually took, next to the Subaru. Two little beeps sounded as we approached. "Nice ride," I said.

"How've you been getting around anyway? Can you drive with that thing?"

"Not really. My car's a stick. Lynne's been bringing me groceries and stuff."

"You two are pretty tight, huh?"

I told him we were.

"You know that guy Speed?"

"He lives in that cabin right over there," I said, gesturing with my head.

"I guess I knew that already," he said quietly.

I wanted to get the skinny on what went down with Lynne and him. I mean, I pretty much knew already, I just wanted to hear it from his point of view. The twenty-one questions could wait until we'd had a couple of drinks though.

Winding down the valley, the road paralleled the Hoback River, with mountains and buttes on either side. This was a direction I hardly ever went. Except to go to Trail Creek. Which had happened only once before, when Jack had gotten a plumbing job and we were feeling flush. Trail Creek was a real locals' joint. I'm not sure what it was like in the summer. Probably got more business from the fly-fishing crowd. But in winter, it was too far from all the action for most people to drive. Like Nora's Fish Creek Inn, if you brought in your catch, they'd fillet it and fry it up for you.

Max put on some Toots & The Maytals—"Pressure Drop"— and from there we said next to nothing on the fifteen-minute drive. He mentioned they'd shot a Marlboro ad down there, and that there were hot springs. That was about it. Both of us, it seemed, were preoccupied with other things, other people. It was kind of a downer too. I mean why should two good people like us have to feel like a couple of friggin' chumps? It wasn't fair.

I recognized Arty, the chef from Anthony's, over at the bar. "Betty, the hell you doin' here?" he called.

We walked over, and I made introductions. Arty had one of

those ZZ Top beards and a long ponytail. He was drinking the usual—a Rusty Nail.

"How come you're not at the Moose?" I asked.

"*You're* not there," he said, his lips curling into a cute smile. Given the hours he worked and his alcohol intake, Arty had every excuse for being a real asshole. Liquor didn't affect him that way though. At least, not that I saw. He was a sweetheart—always good for a kind word. And I couldn't say I'd ever seen him drunk.

He was sizing up the doc. "Where's that rabble-rouser of yours?" he asked.

"Down in Salt Lake," I said.

"When the cat's away, huh?" he joked.

Max put his arm around my shoulder and gave me a squeeze, playing into the couple charade.

"I've gotta have my fun too, you know," I said, going along.

The waitress came over and told us our table was ready. She'd had to set one up special. That's how empty the place was.

"Let me buy you two a drink," Arty said.

"You don't have to do that," Max said.

"A man offers you a drink—"

"Okay. I'd like a Grey Goose martini if they have it."

"Oh sure. They got all the good stuff here, right, Scare Bear?"

An enormous guy with a potbelly was at the other end of the bar, watching a nature channel—herds of hippopotami, basking in swamps somewhere in Africa. "Man, I sure'd like to be where they are right about now," he said.

"You got Grey Goose, don'tcha?"

"Nah, Belvedere," he said, walking over. "Just as good in my opinion."

Scare Bear was the kind of liquor connoisseur you were likely to find in just about any bar in the valley.

"I'll try it. Dirty," Max said. "Betty?"

"Sounds good to me," I said.

A red-and-white checked tablecloth set off by a candle gave Max a healthy glow. We clinked glasses and sipped. "Not bad," he said.

"So what happened with you and Lynne?"

"You have to ask?"

"I could venture a guess, but I wouldn't mind hearing it from the source."

"She dumped me," he said, knitting his fingers and leaning back casually in his chair.

"You sound crushed."

"We hadn't been going out that long," he said. "I never did feel like she was that into it."

I wondered if it would make him feel better to know that she wasn't into *most* guys. "You knew—"

"That she was gay. Yup," he said, nodding his head. "I think I was sort of an experiment."

"Huh." I was halfway through my martini already and feeling pretty loose in the tongue, so I said, "My boyfriend is down in Salt Lake City. With his wife."

"Sounds like a good place for him."

Considering his stand on cheaters, Max probably wasn't the best person to try to have a heart-to-heart with about the situation. I felt like talking about it, but we'd probably have a bet-ter time if I didn't.

After I almost sent my chicken-fried steak flying across the room, Max took my knife and fork and started cutting. It made me feel like a little kid, but it was still pretty sweet of him. I could see he really liked doing stuff like that—taking care of people.

"You're so lucky to have your life all figured out," I said.

"Hardly." He laughed, taking a sip of wine.

"I mean, being a doctor."

"Oh yeah," he said. "That part of it. It's all I ever wanted to be. That and a good husband."

"You're *married*?"

"Was."

"Oh." It was all making sense to me now. "And she cheated on you?"

"Bingo," he said.

"That's not nice."

"No, it isn't."

"Huh."

Where were we supposed to go from there?

"Have you thought about what you want to do? With your life, that is," Max asked, politely changing the topic.

"It's *all* I ever think about anymore," I said. "Somehow, I thought being a ski bum for a while would help me figure it out."

"And it didn't."

"Not really. When I graduated from college, I thought I wanted to make films. *That* never happened."

"Hey, you're not dead yet."

"That's true. I've still got time. It's just so hard to know how to get started."

"In my experience, you start by going out and doing it," he said. "Trial and error. And hard work."

We were in excellent spirits by the time we slid down the icy drive to the cabin. Max put the car into park, left the motor running, got out, opened my door, and watched me slip as my foot hit the ground. "That's it," he said, hoisting me into his arms.

"Watch out for the dog shit." I laughed.

"What, that big, brown thing I just stepped in wasn't a snowball?"

He put me back down on the porch.

"Well, thank you very much for a very pleasant evening," I said.

"The pleasure was all mine," he said, his eyes catching mine.

"You want to come in for a cup of coffee? You've got a long drive home."

"Nah, it's okay. It's getting late. I should get back."

"Suit yourself." I was trying to be casual, but the truth was, I really wanted him to stay.

It must have showed, because he gave me a long look and said, "Oh, who am I kidding, a cup of coffee would be great. Let me run up and kill the engine."

It was nice to have Max there, sitting at the kitchen table, drinking his coffee. I told him I thought Jack might be cheating on me but that, for some reason, I still trusted him. Like, I didn't think he would lie, maybe just not reveal the whole truth about things. Which I suppose is a form of lying.

Max sat, listened, didn't make any judgments. Told me I'd just have to wait and see. Jack was the only one who could clear it up.

Having him there was like a soothing drug. I tried not to think about him going, leaving me there with my own thoughts.

He was on his second cup of coffee when Jim came down to tell me I had a phone call. "A man."

"Jack?"

"Didn't sound like him, and he didn't say hi. . . ."

It was my father. And the news wasn't good. Mom had had another lump biopsied. They'd found cancer.

I'd tried snowboarding one day at the beginning of the season when the conditions were good and hard. Each time I fell backward, it was a full-on body slam to the side of the mountain that took my breath away, leaving me stunned, hurt, and angry. I felt the same way now.

"But I just spoke to her earlier tonight," I said. "Why didn't she tell me?"

"I'm telling you," he said. My father's not a man of many words. "I think you should come home."

chapter 22

Benny picked me up at LaGuardia in his new girlfriend's old, pale yellow Mercedes. "I got into Yale Drama," he said, gunning it onto the highway. "Will you look at this buttwipe? Pull it the fuck *over*. I hate it when those Town Car guys just plant it there like they're still in Puerto Rico or wherever the hell they're from."

"Good for you," I said. Benny had known he wanted to be an actor since dropping football and taking up drama freshman year. I envied him.

"Mom wants me to get an MBA."

"Figures," I said. "How is she?"

"Still a shit disturber," he said, looking over with an arched eyebrow.

"Come on, Benny, you're only fooling *yourself* with this acting business. Let Daddy call Paul Evans over at Credit Suisse."

"That's it!" he said. "Verbatim. I shit you not."

"I bet we won't be hearing any more 'when I die's out of *her*."

"I know. It's enough to make me want to slit my wrists."

In a way, we were joking around because we didn't know how to handle the reality of her condition. "So what's the deal? What are the doctors saying?"

"I think they want to remove one of her breasts. They say if they do that, she'll have a good chance of beating it."

A sharp pain went through my own breast. "God," I said. "How's Dad taking it?"

"He's not saying much. As usual. But I can tell he's losing it a little. He keeps forgetting things, like where he put his keys, his reading glasses, stuff like that. We've been eating a lot of those prepared meals from the Food Emporium. The meat loaf's not bad. I'm doing laundry twenty-four/seven. Since the diagnosis the whole place has fallen apart. You know, with all of that stuff about dying all the time, I really think *she* thought she'd live forever. Secretly, I mean."

I don't know, you would have thought it might feel all right to be home in a way. Even under those circumstances. Like, maybe the sights and sounds of the city—the rush of traffic, the tall buildings springing up from the island of Manhattan in the distance—would bring it all rushing back. Get me all worked up with nostalgia. Instead, I was seized with anxiety. I had to find a job. A shitty, low-level office job most likely, that I'd commute to jammed butt to back on pee-smelling subways like every other sucker in town. There would be pollution to breathe, terrorism to fret about, and my mother, whom I couldn't be pissed at anymore because she might be dying. . . .

Shame overtook me. I should have been focused on Mom, but there I was, true to form, worrying about my own stupid problems.

We passed New Rochelle, Mamaroneck, Rye Brook. Once we hit the Merritt Parkway, things opened up a little, started looking a bit less grim. I had to give it to Connecticut. That stretch of highway was pretty beautiful, pastoral almost. It was a definite contrast to the landscape out west. The hills were small, the vistas, where there were any, less sweeping. It was charming in its own way, just more, I don't know, claustrophobic.

We took Exit 36 and went left on Weed Street. The sign had been stolen by local kids so often, they'd quit replacing it. New Canaan was the American Dream gone haywire. Everywhere you looked you saw the gaudy, gigantic mansions of people who'd made it big. Recently. Not to mention the Hummers, Audis, and Beemers. I could pretend to be appalled and disgusted, but the reality was, compared to most of them, I was a giant zero and knew it.

I wasn't prepared for what I saw when I walked into the kitchen. Mom, who'd been on the plump side since forever, had lost weight. She was standing next to the Sub-Zero, drinking a glass of milk.

"Sweetheart!" She looked exhausted. And happy to see me. It made me glad I came. "Let me look at you! Oh, your wrist. Can I sign your cast?"

"Of course."

Lynne was the only person who'd signed it so far. She'd drawn several upside-down V's for mountains, a small girl skier with pigtails skiing in between, "Mountain Betty" in big block lettering up above.

Dad walked in from the TV room, looking similarly weight deprived, holding his reading glasses. "Hiya, Lizzy," he said, giving me a big hug.

"What's going on around here? You two look like Bergen-Belsen."

"I've been telling your father," Mom said, "cancer is the best diet around."

Things had happened fast. She'd gone in for a routine examination and was scheduled to have her breast removed two days later. The night before she had to go in, I watched her polish off nearly a whole bottle of Chardonnay and smoke a single cigarette. She'd quit ten years before. No one said anything. Not even Dad, who was prone to calling her on stuff. Now that she might really be dying, not just threatening to, Mom had carte blanche to do whatever she wanted. And just when I was ready and willing to listen to every criticism she'd ever leveled— listen and reform on the spot, make a vow of celibacy if need be—it was like she'd taken a resignation pill and had only nice things to say. She sat at the dusty piano in the library and played scales for the first time in years.

I was glued to the TV, watching reruns of Law & Order, muting the volume to hear her play Mozart, the way she had when I was a kid. For years I'd thought of my mother only in relation to myself. Now it occurred to me that she had her own inner life— her own fears and anxieties.

Jerry Orbach and Benjamin Bratt ran down the street after a

young black kid while Mom poured it out. This wasn't Eagle's Rest or Après Vous, where I could make everything better by repeating "Weight on the downhill ski." I thought about the mental and the physical and wondered if perhaps Mom hadn't *given* herself cancer. Like, if you think about dying all the time, maybe you're sort of killing yourself in a way.

After the operation, Dad called from Sloan-Kettering to tell us it had gone well. I thought of how maddeningly judgmental Mom could be, all weak, skinny, and sorely one-breasted in some sterile hospital bed somewhere.

Did any of it matter now? Any of it at all?

On the morning after Mom got her first dose of chemo, I made her a couple of eggs just the way she liked them—soft-boiled, chopped up and oozing in the bowl with warm pieces of toast, sprinkled with olive oil, balsamic vinegar, salt and pepper. Warming the milk for her coffee on the stove, I tried to whisk in a little foam to remind her of her vacation with Dad in Paris the summer before. I lined a tray with a white Irish linen napkin embroidered with flowers and arranged everything as invitingly as possible. It was still missing something. Grabbing a pair of Fiskars from one of the kitchen drawers, I ran out to the pond and looked for the sprightliest daffodil I could find.

Mom took one look at it all and with a weak smile said, "Oh, Elizabeth, how lovely."

I cleared the magazines and old water glasses off her bedside table and laid the tray down, shook out a linen napkin, and tucked it under her chin. Spooning up a bit of egg and toast, I held it up to her mouth and said, "Mmmm, good," like you would if you were feeding a baby.

Mom's lip began trembling. "I'm sorry, dear, I can't."

Within a week, the whole Winters family (except Benny, who was in love) looked like *Dawn of the Dead*, walking around the house in ratty old robes and threadbare sweats, slippers that looked like they'd been gnawed on by dogs we didn't have.

There was endless laundry to do, rugs to vacuum, plants to water, groceries to purchase. . . . I tried to be as helpful as I could, and I know it must have made a difference, but it didn't feel that way.

The day I got my cast off, a letter from Jack arrived in the mailbox. Despite letters upside down and backward, I managed to decipher, and I'll paraphrase, that he'd never been more sorry about anything in his life but that he wanted me to know, he'd slept with someone else since I'd been gone. Who it was wasn't important. *She* wasn't important to him. I was. He missed me, and promised that when I got back, everything would be better again.

Talk about a "Dear Betty." I think it's almost worse when a person cheats on you yet still claims to love you. I mean, what are you supposed to say to *that?* And why, for fuck's sake, is betrayal so alluring? Why did pain and rejection only make me want Jack more? Looked like I'd have to change my definition of love. Because I wasn't sure how much more my heart could take.

Mom's cancer had taken its toll already. I'd had moments over the past couple of weeks when I'd thought I might just stay. But the *letter*. Maybe it was an ego thing or something, but I just couldn't take the fact that he'd actually gone ahead and done it. He, who during moments of drunken fuzziness had sat on a barstool repeating "I love you Betty" over and over so many times that I'd wondered if there wasn't something seriously wrong with him.

I called Lynne. Asked her what she knew. She said she didn't know anything, but given his history I might have expected it, right? I told her I was an idiot. But that wasn't too helpful in terms of cheering me up. She said there were plenty of fish in the sea and asked me when I was coming back to Jackson. She had a present for me. I didn't ask but had a feeling she'd gone out and splurged on some new telly gear. I told her I didn't know.

I was curled up in my childhood bed, staring up at the star and planet glow-in-the-dark decals on the ceiling, thinking what the pink room needed was a paint job. Something less cheery— black or blood red perhaps. I'd gotten my cast off the day before and my arm looked pale and shriveled, the hair darker and more plentiful. Benny and his girlfriend, Mia, were downstairs making lasagna. It smelled fantastic, but I was still going to need a glass of wine to get the old appetite cranking.

We were waiting to hear the latest from Mom's doctors. The phone rang. I didn't move. Benny called from downstairs. "Someone named *Malarial* wants to talk to you!"

I picked up the faux old-fashioned receiver in my parents'
bedroom. "Hello?"

"Bet-ty."

"Muriel."

"I heerd about what has happened."

And now you're calling to tell me you told me so.

"I jes taught, maybe you want to talk?" she said.

She didn't sound angry, vengeful, or drunk. She wasn't
gloating either.

"Because we go trew seemeelair teeng? Ah?"

"Who told you?"

"Jack. He luv you. He told me. But you know, ee told me ee
luv me too. I want you to know. He cannot elp heemself, ah?
Eets de way ee ees."

"I know," I said, my voice nasally from crying so much. And I
did know. It was weird. I mean, I'd been cheated on before, and
in each instance, I wound up utterly hating the guy. But with
Jack, I felt different. Because I honestly *believed* he was inca-
pable of being any other way. He would be like that for the rest
of his life, and thinking he'd be any different with me was just
a stupid, egotistical pipe dream. It was why I'd been drawn
to him, I guess, and why I knew ultimately, somewhere deep
down, it would have to end. And that made me nothing so
much as sorry.

The waterworks really started going then. I was sort of letting it all out and holding it all in at the same time. "You know
my mother has cancer?" I said.

"I deedn't know," she said. "My fadder ave, *had* it too."

"What kind of cancer did he have?"

"Leever."

"I'm sorry," I said.

"Your mudder, what does she ave?"

"Breast."

Body parts. They're part of us, yet it's possible to live without some of them. "She had a mastectomy."

"Je suis desolé. She's okay now?" Muriel asked.

"I don't know."

"You need to talk, you call me, ah? You don go trew eet alone like eye deed."

"Okay."

Back in bed, in an old pair of underwear and a sweatshirt, I began reading *The Adventures of Huckleberry Finn*. The more I tried to force myself to get into the story, the less I was able to concentrate. The book was falling apart too, the pages yellow and frayed, ripping slightly from the binding each time I turned one. Goddamnit. Sticking my knobby legs into a pair of sweats, I headed down to the kitchen.

The marble island was covered with mozzarella, eggs, ricotta, tomatoes, cooked meat, and spinach. Benny sat at the kitchen table reading *The Cherry Orchard* while Mia stood by the sink over a colander separating lasagna noodles. I didn't say anything about the mess, but they could bet their sweet asses I would if they didn't clean up.

"Hey," Mia said, concentrating on her task.

"Hey," I said.

Benny didn't look up from his book.

"Aren't you going to say *hey*?" I asked.

"Hey, hey, hay is for horses," Benny said, still not looking up.

Opening the fridge, I rooted in and around old Glad-wrapped onion halves, olives in a festering brine, two-month-date-past-due sour cream, shriveled strawberries, disintegrating parsley, moldy lemons, and Tupperware with tiny remnants of dinners past, searching in vain for a bottle of sparkling water. I'd like to say the sloppy status of the fridge was brought on by extraordinary circumstances, but the truth is, that fridge (the entire kitchen, to be *perfectly* truthful) is always in need of a serious makeover, and the only time it gets one is when I'm home.

Dragging the garbage pail over, I began tossing things out, emptying the side storage areas of ketchup, horseradish, soy sauce, mustard, and mayo, throwing away anything that looked familiar from the last time I'd gone through.

Clearing a spot on the counter, I lined up returnable items, such as milk, cream, and orange juice, so I could wipe down the glass shelves with a sponge, using the green, Brillo-y side to scrape off driplets of yogurt, sauce, cheese, dried milk, and juice. As for the drawers strewn with papery garlic, shallot, and onion skins, I'd take them to the big sink down in the basement for a full-on spray and scrub.

Slipping past Mia, who it's fair to say, looked every bit the young Claudia Schiffer, her long, blond hair stuck into a messy yet somehow gorgeous bun on top of her head, I grabbed a wad of Bounty from the roll hanging by the side of the sink.

Benny's girlfriends were always drop-dead. Whether she could cook or not was a different story.

"Excuse me," I said, reaching into the cupboard around her magnificent stems for the 409. We all might be going to hell in a handbasket, but by God, that fridge was going to sparkle!

On the bits that would not come off with either the green side of the sponge or the 409, I used my fingernail, letting the schmeg gather until the end, when I could focus, with the metal nail file attachment on the clippers.

"Is now really the best time to be doing that?" Benny asked.

I didn't answer for a full minute and considered not answering at all, such was my hair across.

"Betty?"

I stopped scrubbing a moment. "*What, Benny?*" Boy was I feeling righteous. How dare he tell me what to do? *Me,* so clean, helpful, and holy? "Do you really want to go on *living* this way?" I asked, not exactly sure what I was talking about.

"Living *what* way?" he replied. And don't think I didn't catch him smiling over at Mia like I was a deranged midget.

"Like this!" I said, sweeping my hand toward the fridge and counter.

"We're going to clean up," he said.

"You mean *Mia's* going to clean up."

"Right." He was still smiling.

"You are such a pig," I said, my anger beginning to overwhelm me. "What is *with* you anyway? Do you think you can just sit there reading Chekhov while the world falls to shit around you?"

I hadn't meant to cry. In fact, I thought it was all kind of funny in a tragic way. Benny and Mia came over and put their arms around me. "Shhh, it's okay," they said. "We'll clean up. Everything's going to be all clean, sparkly clean, don't worry."

Talk about melodrama. I'd turned into a regular Bette Davis. Through my laughy, hiccupy sniffles I said, "Cleanliness is close to godliness."

"Yeah, and if anything happens to Mom, that guy's going to be on my shit list," Benny said.

On the day I got the letter from Jack, even though we'd been talking twice a day at appointed times, he suddenly became hard to reach. I went crazy. Why did he have to tell me at all? He knew what I was going through. Who knows. He was probably scared I'd find out from someone else. Isn't that the only reason anyone ever cops to anything?

His voice, when I finally got him on the line, sounded distant, sad, and uncommunicative. My queries—who was the little slut? What did the bitch look like? Did she give him better blow jobs?—were met with stony silence. I hated myself for stooping to such jaded displays. These were not questions Jack was apt to answer.

The only detail I got from him was that she was petite, and had short, blond hair. Definitely enough for me to work with. I watched his chest flush red, the way it did when he made love to me, and imagined it did the same exact thing when he fucked the Tiny One—*whoever* she was.

He asked when I was coming home. I told him I wasn't sure I was. He said he was thinking of moving down to Salt Lake early to start training. I told him to go ahead. He should do what he needed to do. "But then again"—I couldn't resist—"you've already done that, haven't you?"

By the time the doctors finally announced they were "cautiously optimistic" about Mom's condition, it was the middle of March. It's a tricky month because the weather's usually miserable, yet hope's on the horizon since April, May, and summer are just around the bend. I think it makes everyone a little schizoid.

Living in the house with my parents, knowing how they felt about where I'd been, what I'd done, who I was with, yet unable to hate them for it anymore was almost more than I could stand. So when Jack said he was coming east to sort things out, I knew we would have to go somewhere else. I also knew that I would have to lie to my parents about it. Something I didn't *want* to do but seemed wholly unable to avoid.

I told them I would be going into New York City for a couple of days to hang with Georgia, an old college friend, who, as we all knew, had been busting her hump ever since graduation, rising through the ranks of the ad biz. Sometimes I thought my parents might prefer having a go-getter like her as their daughter. She wouldn't go running off with her ne'er-do-well boyfriend and lie about it so soon after her mother had been delivered from death's door.

Improbable as it now seems, part of me thought that if Jack and I just moved somewhere else, we might be able to work through it all. Maybe someplace where we could have real jobs, hang out with ambitious people who didn't have time to smoke pot, snort coke, and cheat on their girlfriends all day. Like another city or town would turn us into different people. I thought if I could just get him to fall in love with the East Coast, we might have a chance.

A surge of relief went through me when I saw Jack walk through the gate. This initial reaction was quickly followed by the pain, anger, and humiliation of his betrayal. So while part of me yearned to throw him down on the thin airport rug just to show him and everyone else he was mine, the other part wanted to smack him silly. And still another wanted to melt away, like the Wicked Witch of the West does when she gets doused with water.

He came directly over, dropped his bag, and hugged me fiercely, as though he would never, ever, let me go. When we pulled back from each other, his eyes were red and damp. He said, "I love you, Betty. Don't you ever forget that."

Strong words from a guy who couldn't keep his dick in his pants. *Anyhoo.* I *wanted* to believe him, which in many ways made it easier to.

The plan was, we would drive up to North Conway, New Hampshire and stay in a B & B. It was cold, rainy, and gray. I hadn't made reservations anywhere but was sure we'd be able to get something on the fly. I'd chosen New Hampshire because Jack had never been east before and I wanted to impress him, show him we had mountains here too.

As we got off the highway and things started getting all "ye ole shoppe," Jack became even more maudlin, if that was possible. The two of us stared puffy-eyed through the windshield in silence, mostly. It wasn't your usual postcheating exchange—threats and accusations, lying about how you'll make it up, etcetera. It was pure, unadulterated misery. If Jack were more savvy, you might think his ability to come off so hurt and upset was some kind of manipulation tactic. But he wasn't a schemer, and it didn't take a genius to see he hated himself for what he'd done.

Okay, so maybe *hate* is too strong a word. I mean, he probably didn't experience too much self-loathing when he was throwing it to Tiny. Let's just say, he certainly put on a good show.

The charming New England countryside was not working its magic on *him*, that was for sure. Each time we passed an antiques store, he'd hold up his finger like a gun and make that explosion sound.

We stopped at several B & Bs, all of which either were too expensive or didn't have any rooms available. Finally, a gas station attendant sent us to the hostel up at Pinkham Notch. It was cheap, and they might have room, this being the off-season and all.

Up past Santa's Village, and the Conway Scenic Railroad we went, into and out of the mist, the rain turning to snow, hail, then back to rain again. The heater in Mia's car worked sporadically, so that by the time we pulled into the lot, the cold had seeped into our bones.

Jack plastered himself to me, his arm over my shoulder as we stood shivering, watching the young guy at the front desk stare at availabilities on his computer screen. "We just got a school group in this morning. Usually we're not this full. . . . Looks like there's a room for four with two bunk beds. You might have to share," he said, looking up.

"You don't have anything private?" I asked. I mean, shit, Jack and I needed our own space to cry, bargain, make promises we couldn't keep, and generally carry on.

We checked out the room, which was small, dark, and already occupied by two other people. I stopped into the communal bathroom to take a leak and splash water on my eyes, which were caked and stinging with tear salt.

Back down at the front desk, we waited while the guy went through other nearby options. "You might try the Iron Mountain Hotel. You passed it on the way up from North Conway."

"Is it inexpensive?" I asked.

"I've never stayed there myself, but I think so," he said.

"Are you talking about that big place with the chipped paint and the crumbling front porch?" Jack asked.

"You saw it?" I asked.

"Yeah, I saw it," Jack grumbled. "It looks haunted."

"You might not have much of a choice at this hour," the guy said, checking his watch.

I hate it when I don't plan properly and things don't just *fall into place*. We'd been driving forever and were so tired we could have crashed standing up.

"Come on, Betty, let's go check it out."

"You guys have sleeping bags, you can stay out in one of the huts," the guy said in a last-ditch effort.

"Nah, we didn't bring our camping gear," Jack said.

We were out of our element. Driving around in a borrowed car, no mattress, no sleeping bags, no gun. . . . It made us feel like a couple of numskulls. And who knows, maybe we were.

Back down the road we went. "Hey, wasn't that it?" Jack asked.

Slowing down, I pulled the Mercedes over, the rain, snow, and hail magnified in the headlights as darkness fell. Putting the car into reverse, we rolled back past the drive. *"Caramba,"* I said.

"We should check it out," Jack said.

Young couple in a Mercedes pulls up to the creepy hotel . . .

An orange light diffused by cigarette smoke glowed from inside the tiny office. A large silver bell sat next to an open guest book. Jack rang it. We waited as the cigarette smoke continued to waft out from behind the front desk. "Hello?" I said. "Anyone here?"

The place was silent except for the hot water heater, the distant sound of a running shower.

Lifting up the wood partition, I stuck my head inside the office. Slumped in a ripped BarcaLounger slept a shriveled old man. Clamped between two yellow fingers was the filter of a cigarette, the ash, nearly four inches of it, looked like the Leaning Tower of Pisa.

"Hello?" I said, in a soft voice. And again, louder, "Hel-lo-ho!"

The old man jerked up, his rheumy eyes slowly coming into focus. "What? Who's there?" he asked, confused.

"Hi," I said. "We're looking for a room?"

"What type of room you looking for?"

"Something with a queen-size bed preferably," I said.

"We got one a those. Sign the guest book."

"How much will it cost?" I asked, pulling out the remainder of the grocery money Dad had given me.

"Twenty dollars a night."

"The price is right," Jack said.

Just then, the smoke from inside the office began puffing out in thick clouds.

"Is something on fire back there?" I asked.

Tilting his head slightly, the old man averted his eyes. "Nah. Don't think so." He spoke in a clipped New Hampshire accent.

"You might want to check a little harder," Jack said.

Turning from the desk, the old man shuffled back toward the inner office. After some knocking, paper shuffling, book dropping, and lounger smacking, the smoke abated and he came back out.

"All set?" I asked.

"Eee-yuh," he said.

Jack looked resigned. "Could you give us a minute?" I asked, dragging Jack by the sleeve over to the door.

"Go ahead," the old man called. "Discuss it amongst yourselves."

"We can't stay here," I said.

"Where else are we going to stay, Betty? It's almost eight o'clock."

"That old geezer's going to fall asleep with a lit cigarette and burn this place down in the middle of night."

I'd like to say this was the first time I'd ever found myself stuck up shit creek, but the truth is, stuff like that happens to me all the time.

"Excuse me, sir?" Jack called. "Did one of your cigarettes start a fire?"

"You might say," the old man said, raising an eyebrow.

Fact was, it was all the same to him whether we decided to stay the night or not.

"We going to have to worry about this place burning down in the middle of night?" Jack asked.

"Great," I said. "Ask him."

"Might," said the old man, cracking what looked like a smile.

"Come on, Betty, the weather's getting worse," Jack said, signing us in as Jack and Betty Catcher.

If the place did burn down in the middle of the night, I reasoned, at least it would put us out of our misery.

The bed was lumpy, the sheets threadbare, but it was, as the old man said, a queen. Opening the closet, I half expected a decaying skeleton to come flying out. The bathroom was down at the end of the hall. It's a good thing we had provisions—a tin of smoked oysters, another of kippered snacks, a summer sausage, a box of Triscuits, a lemon, a couple of cans of Fresca, and a bottle of Absolut. After spreading it all out on the nubbly white bedspread, we stared at it awhile. We weren't hungry even though we hadn't eaten anything but a couple of sausage-and-egg McMuffins all day.

"Think there's an ice machine?" Jack asked.

We both started to laugh.

"Yeah, right next to the pool and spa," I said.

We stopped then. Jack said, "I don't know if I'll ever be able to be the kind of guy you want me to be, Betty."

I just love it when guys say crap like that. Put their inability to be a stand-up guy on *your* shoulders. As if expecting them to keep their weenies clean is just *too* much to ask.

"You mean, the kind of guy who doesn't fuck around?"

"If you hadn't left, it wouldn't have happened."

"Are you telling me you can't be on your own for three weeks, while I'm with my mother, who has cancer, without going out and screwing some *petite blonde*?"

He hung his head.

"I don't understand. Am I supposed to feel sorry for *you* here or what?"

He shook his head and said, "I've already said I'm sorry. What more do you want me to say?"

"I don't know, Jack." March was working its schizophrenic

magic—I wanted him, I hated him, I was angry, I felt guilty about it. . . . The situation was impossible. It had become evident (in a nebulous sort of way), as Jack poured warm drinks into plastic cups, that we were destined for nothing greater than Iron Mountain living. It didn't matter where we moved.

We didn't sleep much in the lumpy bed that night. And not because we were going at it like monkeys either. The sex, what there was of it, was the consoling kind—sad and a little bit desperate.

We spent the majority of the next day in bed too, and the crappy weather wasn't the only reason why. I think somewhere deep down we knew we weren't going to be together anymore. By the end of the weekend, we were so brokenhearted that even though it was impossible to imagine parting, there was some comfort in the idea of starting over alone.

On the drive back down to New York, we found a steak joint and sat at a dark little table drinking Absolut on the rocks with twists. I was so malnourished, a few sips went straight to my head. As I sat letting an ice cube melt between clenched teeth, Jack pulled a small box from his pocket and slid it across the table. "I had a friend in Salt Lake make it for you," he said.

"Oh no" escaped, and I clamped my hand over my mouth.

Underneath the little square of cotton padding wasn't, as I'd feared, an engagement ring, but a pinkie ring embedded with tiny diamonds and turquoise. Even though it didn't look too expensive, I knew Jack couldn't afford it. It was the only piece of jewelry he'd ever given me, the type of gesture he knew I'd like. And as he slipped it onto my finger, it felt less like a symbol of our love and friendship, more like something to remember him by.

Jack had the rib eye, I had the tenderloin with béarnaise and a baked potato on the side. I got through most of it too, Jack having somehow become an appetite enhancer. What we didn't finish, we had the waiter pack to go. I wound up holding on to that aluminum-foiled swan for weeks, as sort of a meat memento.

chapter 25

Cracking open an eye to a flash of pink wallpaper, I thought, for an instant, that the whole trip to New Hampshire had been a bad dream. No such luck. I really was single, unemployed, and living with my parents. Pulling on a pair of sweats, I stuck my hair up in an elastic and headed down to the kitchen. Dad had already left for work, Benny was over at Mia's, and Mom was still asleep. I decided to take a walk.

The air was damp, and the monotone hue of the sky made it feel colder, in every possible respect, than the temperature, the macadam on pristine Cherry Blossom Lane marred by patches of moisture. Out on the main road, I stayed as far over to the side as I could each time one of those urban assault vehicles threatened to flatten me like the scum of the earth I was.

During the five-mile loop, which in happier times I ran, I was joined by a sweet black Lab. Sweet, that is, until he picked up the dead carcass of a squirrel, ran ahead, plopped it down in my path, and began munching on the bone and cartilage. *That, I thought, is life.* Call me depressed. Call me a little whiner. What did I care? How *low* can you *go?* Shit, I couldn't even get my ass *near* the limbo stick.

The hum of an engine approached, the decibels increasing from behind. I leapt into the pachysandra, nearly tripping on one of the many beer bottles and cans that were surprisingly prevalent in that neck of the woods. The X5 passed and slowed. Up on the hill, the brake lights came on. For a minute my heart jumped into my throat. *Max?* I said aloud.

The SUV kept going.

The Lab gave me a pitying look, affirming I was, indeed, every bit the loser we all suspected, before picking up the dead squirrel and moving on to greener pastures.

Several days of very serious mulling ensued. What I needed was money. Without it, I was no one, nothing. And it would do no good to make a nickel here, a dime there. No, I needed a *career.* An honorable pursuit. One that would utilize all of my talents. *Whatever* they were. Something that would serve me well in the days, weeks, months, and years to come. I wanted, no *needed,* to do the right thing. There would be no more wake and bakes, no more shots of tequila, or gunslinging, or sex with married men, or messing around on mountains. I had a new mountain to climb—a mountain of the *soul.* In short, there would be no more fun of any kind in the foreseeable future. My wild days were over.

It's a testament to my total lack of imagination that the only stable, moneymaking careers that jumped to mind were medicine and law, neither of which I'd ever shown a lick of interest in or talent for, but which seemed like safe bets.

Dad thought we might more rapidly get to the bottom of the pressing question of what I was going to do with the rest of my life by having my aptitudes tested at a place he'd gone twenty-five-odd years previous to have his aptitudes tested. I couldn't argue with success.

Mom provided a dress suit, stockings, work bag for important documents and papers I didn't have, and a sensible pair of Talbots flats. I hadn't looked so official in years.

Dad passed his copy of The New York Times over to me like a baton, and the three of us, Dad, Mom, and I, got into their Range Rover and drove to the station. I took my rightful seat on the Metro-North connector, looking every bit the New Canaan go-getter. I pulled out my dog-eared (and it has to be said, given the time it took to read, incredibly thick) copy of Atlas Shrugged and my parents waved as the train pulled out of the station, bell ringing.

Moving slowly past the town tennis courts, I peered up briefly to assess new cargo at Talmadge Hill, Springdale, Glen-brook, and Stamford. Sitting with the paper and book on my lap, cracking open neither, I daydreamed about an illustrious future as I stared out the window, watching the brown water of the sound, blue bridges, highways, graffiti, and projects pass by. As soon as everything went dark, I knew we were closing in on Grand Central Terminal.

* * *

Johnson O'Connor was located in a big, vine-covered brown-
stone. A wrought-iron gate opened onto a small courtyard,
flat stones cutting a path to enormous glass doors likewise
adorned, reassuringly, with iron.

A pleasant-looking girl with a brunette bob greeted me at
the door. She looked about my age but had a job. And a job
suddenly seemed like the most impossible and desirable thing
to have. "Employment" had become this exclusive club that I
wanted desperately to join. Smiling and holding out her hand,
she introduced herself as Gwen. I told her my name was Elizabeth, which she already knew because I had an appointment.
I wasn't dropping in for scones and clotted cream . . . and I
wasn't Betty. Not anymore.

The testing was to go on for three days, after which the ex-
perts at Johnson O'Connor would sit me down and give it to me
straight. I, of course, had my own ideas about what I wanted to
hear. Law and medicine were at the top of "our" list.

As I followed Gwen up the grand winding staircase to the
second floor, the smell of the wood, mixed with the polish on
the linoleum floors on the landing, made me think of junior
high. I wondered if the water in the child-height fountain
would taste similarly soft and metallic. She wore black penny
loafers, a sensible midcalf-length navy linen skirt with matching jacket, and a white silk blouse. She looked like she had
what it would take to figure me out.

Opening one of the doors on the long second-floor hallway,

Gwen led me into a small, white room with a desk and two chairs, positioned side by side. There would be no power plays here, no interviewer-interviewee scenario. She asked a few rudimentary questions without delving too deep. That was what the tests were for.

As Gwen described it, they'd be examining a wide array of aptitudes to find out whether I was detail oriented, good for, say, investigative work and *law*, or more of a generalist, someone who'd be better at seeing the big picture, a manager perhaps. She was very nice. Smiled and had a good attitude. Somewhere in there I found out she was studying for her master's in social psychology. She was a *can do* girl.

Once the pleasantries were over with, Gwen said, "Let the games begin!" pulled out a stopwatch, and timed me as I attempted to put small pegs into tiny holes—the test for manual dexterity, good, she explained, for working on factory assembly lines and surgical procedures alike. I was glad to know they weren't testing strictly for white-collar aptitudes. Although I really didn't want to be told my destiny was to work at a cannery or on some kind of assembly line. But surgeon? Now we're talking. Maybe all those years of violin would finally pay off.

Next, she brought out a large black notebook containing pages of various images—a fireman, corncob, police car, baby, dog, house. While she flipped pages, I was supposed to glance and, as quickly as I could, tell her what had changed. Was the corncob bigger? The fireman smaller? The house missing altogether?

Chewing on a finger, eyes darting over the page, I found my head was clouded where *Jeopardy!* quickness was called for.

A pair of old-fashioned, rubbery earphones materialized to test for tone, rhythm, and pitch. Was the sound higher or lower? Flat or major? Now clap back the beat . . .

When I asked for the topic of the creative writing sample, Gwen said, "No topic, you can write about anything you want, just don't stop writing for ten minutes. If you can manage it, don't let your pen leave the page."

Regurgitating my innermost thoughts? *Glad you asked.* As I recall, I wrote mostly about the experience of being at Johnson O'Connor and how surreal it was to be there in that grand, old building like my father before me, getting tested on things I should have already known the answers to. I was a late bloomer. Didn't get my period until I was almost sixteen. It took me longer to figure things out than most people. I envied the ones who knew what they wanted to be since they were six or five or four, and conducted their lives accordingly.

On the third day, the day I was to receive my evaluation, I wore a Norma Kamali pantsuit (and makeup!) so that I might march from the building in style and immediately embark on a series of job interviews.

What I got from Gwen was "You did extremely well on the tone, pitch, and rhythm segments of the test."

I couldn't think of a single job that might correspond, but I tried to stay cheerful. Here it was, the moment I'd been waiting for. The suspense was killing me.

She paused for a moment before asking, "Do you play a musical instrument?"

"I played the violin for twelve years," I said. I wanted to add "My mother forced me and I hated it" but kept my mouth shut.

"Our recommendation would be that you continue practicing a musical instrument of some sort."

This did not strike me as particularly helpful career advice. "I've been meaning to take up guitar," I offered, thinking of Curly and the Stagecoach Band.

"Excellent! You are definitely a person that needs music in her life."

Having music in my life sounded great, but a girl can't live on music alone. I wanted to know where the bread was going to come from. "And what jobs coincide with that?" I asked, uncertainly.

"Well, plenty of jobs incorporate music to varying degrees. For instance, advertising has jingles . . ."

"Huh. You think I could be a jingle writer?"

"Why not?"

Gwen was starting to look like less of an authority than I'd originally given her credit for.

"But let's not stop there. You also did incredibly well on the creative writing portion of the test."

"All that crap?" I blurted. "It was just incoherent blabbering!"

"Oh, far from it!" she cried, attempting to remain upbeat. "We suggest you go into a creative field."

This was not what I wanted to hear. "Such as?"

"Well, advertising for one."

Advertising. I rolled the word around on my tongue. It didn't taste too good. "What if I'm morally opposed to advertising?"

Gwen smiled. "There will always be something about a job

you don't like, even if you're using your aptitudes to their fullest."

I had an overwhelming urge to slap her. "Okay, don't laugh," I said. "How about private investigating? Or like, law, or the CIA?" I'd secretly fantasized about undergoing a *La Femme Nikita* transformation, but I wasn't about to trot out my gun skills, and they sure as shit weren't testing for them.

"This area was not your strength."

"What, just because I couldn't figure out whether the corn-cob was bigger?"

"You don't have to yell," Gwen said, trying to maintain a semblance of calm. "Private investigation requires a good bit of organization, an eye for detail. Your scores in this area were below average. Ditto the CIA and law," she said sorrowfully, running her pencil down the graph paper that presumably held the key to my future.

"What about medicine?" I inquired hopefully. After all, I could truss a turkey and fillet a fish like nobody's business. I was sure I could work miracles on a cadaver. "I mean, surgery. I think I'd be really good at that."

"Well, you didn't perform too well on the manual dexterity tests either."

Good God. What the hell was I qualified for?

"And looking at your college and high school transcripts, I noticed you didn't take a single science class after tenth-grade biology."

"So? Couldn't I go back to school and take the classes I'd need?"

"You could," she said, like that would in no way be a good idea, "but you'd need several more years before you could apply to medical schools."

Several more years of school sounded right up my alley. The longer I could put off this career thing, the better. "There's always night school. I could work hard . . ."

Pity overtook Gwen's face.

"Can you throw out any other possibilities? I mean, is jingle writing my lot in life?"

"Oh, God no! By all means no! There's marketing and PR, and well, you didn't hear it from me, but you could always try to be a musician in your spare time." She said this last part like we were partners in crime.

I envisioned myself all grunged out in beads, jeans, and a headband, swilling Southern Comfort straight from the bottle like Janis Joplin, or copping a mean heroin habit like Keith Richards. At that point, I felt so defeated the vision held a certain amount of charm. Unfortunately, I was about as far from being a musician as I was from becoming a doctor. In addition, it was not something I could proudly bring the 'rents. Especially after Dad had plunked down his hard-earned money to get me all tested and squared away. I could just see it now. "Mom? Dad? It looks like I'm going to be a rock star!"

It would kill them.

"I'm definitely going to look into guitar," I said.

"That's the spirit!"

I started to panic. I mean, PR? Marketing? What did those things even *mean*?

I'd like to say the city worked its old magic on me—the way

it had when I was sixteen, drinking Manhattans at Elaine's with my girlfriends on our fathers' dimes. How frivolous we'd been, hailing cabs to take us several short blocks, buying dresses for the Gold and Silver Ball at the Hyatt, where we'd rent rooms with our boyfriends, pretending we were older, more sophisticated and mature. Little did *we* know. It was only six short years later, and somehow I felt I knew less about myself than I had back then. I was fairly certain nothing would please my parents more than for me to move back permanently, get a stable job in an office somewhere, date an eligible guy or two. But as I walked back to Grand Central station, inhaling the exhaust, the Talbots flats gnawing away at my feet, I wasn't at all sure I was cut out for it.

Back at the kitchen table, studying the tristate area in a road atlas, I tried to ascertain where some serious outdoor recreation could be had. New Paltz had the Gunks for climbing, and there was mountain biking in Minnewaska State Park. Not exactly Yellowstone National.

"Johnson O'Connor should be used strictly as a guide," Dad said when I gave him the grim news about my low scores on the corncob test. "They're not the holy grail. You can still apply to law school. I could give Bill Carney a call over at Cravath. You could get your feet wet as a paralegal."

"Right," I said, sipping a mug of chai. I didn't want to appear ungrateful, but the lack of mountains close by, major ones that you could climb, ski, and cycle, was bringing me down. I'd been back east for a little over a month, and I felt like the proverbial fish out of water, flopping around on the dock, gills straining. I was suffocating.

"With this recession," Mom added, "you'd be lucky to have it."

"Exactly," I agreed, heading down to the basement to WD-40 the chain and pump up the tires of my old Fuji. All of my gear—skis, mountain bike, road bike, my limbs as it were—was still back in Jackson in Lynne's parents' basement. But it didn't look like I'd be getting back there to pick it up anytime soon. And that thought depressed me as much as, if not more than, anything had over the past few weeks.

As Mom's health improved, I began to feel more and more trapped in a life that was being prescribed for me. It wasn't that I didn't appreciate everything Mom and Dad were doing. On one level, I was excited to head out into the "real world" and make a decent wage. It was more of an inkling—the way I couldn't wait to wash my face as soon as I applied makeup, or how my legs felt like sausages in stockings, or the blisters on blisters I got from even the most innocuous dress shoes—that the office life, and law in particular (as Johnson O'Connor had astutely pointed out), probably wasn't for me.

It was the beginning of April. The Jackson Hole Pole Pedal Paddle, a race that combined skiing, cycling, and river transport, was happening in a week. Lynne and Speed were planning on taking home the prize this year.

I couldn't help comparing everything I saw to where I'd come from. I was homesick for Rendezvous Bowl, the Hobacks, Snow King, Slide Mountain, Jenny Lake, Granite Canyon, the Sleeping Indian, the Moose. I thought of the hike up to Amphitheater Lake that Lynne and I did last summer. How we'd gone skinny-dipping in the clear, freezing water to cool off and had to start hiking again fast to warm up. There was the 4:00 A.M. climb up the Grand Teton itself. If God was anywhere, it was there, in those cool, running rivers and smooth, steep dirt. Summer in Jackson was even better than winter, and summer was on its way.

Generally, I started feeling more optimistic in the spring, like I was getting a new lease on life. This year, it felt like I was throwing in the towel. It was the end of an era, and while I was thankful Mom was doing better, I wasn't at all sure I liked what was coming down the pike.

Upon returning from a meditative five miler, on which I'd entertained myself by putting all the crap I found along the side of the road into a garbage bag, I collected the various papers sheathed in blue plastic littered at the foot of the drive and checked the box for yesterday's mail. The only and last letter I'd personally received was the "Dear Betty" from Jack, so I wasn't expecting the thin envelope addressed to me in neat block lettering. There was no return address.

Ripping it open, I saw that the handwritten note began:

Dear Betty Winters,
I have been trying to get in touch with you since my recovery and
subsequent transformation . . .

Now before I go any further, let me just say, I am not a religious person, but I'm not exactly an agnostic anymore either. I believe that there is a God and that miracles do happen. I also believe we never know what's in store, so we've got to keep the faith, because there *will* be moments of joy worth living for.

In short, Cecil Black thanked me for my discretion, teaching him to parallel, and saving his life . . . in that order. He asked that I not contact him.

Enclosed was my tip—a cashier's check for one hundred thousand dollars.

My heart started palpitating so wildly I almost had a coronary myself, right there on my parents' front lawn. This had to be some kind of joke. The check couldn't be real.

Running into the house, I nailed my shin on the stairs and limped into my parents' bedroom, where Mom was resting. Or, more accurately, reading *People*. Sitting on the edge of the bed, unable to speak, I handed her the check.

"Is this one of those Publishers Clearing House things?" she asked, inspecting it.

I shook my head, gripping the duvet cover with my sweaty fingers.

"Who on *earth* is Cecil Black?"

"One of my old clients."

"*Clients?*"

"When I was a prostitute," I said. "I thought you knew."

"Don't joke."

"I gave him skiing lessons. I sort of saved his life. I might have saved his marriage, it's hard to tell by the letter," I said, passing it over to her.

"You *sort of* saved his life?" Plumping up a pillow, she leaned forward, adjusted her reading glasses, and said, "Would you mind?"

I arranged the pillows behind her so she could sit up more comfortably.

"That's perfect," she said, as she began to read. When she'd finished, she handed the letter back and said, "I'm sorry, dear, I'm confused. You *actually* saved someone's life? How come you never mentioned it?"

"I don't know," I said. "It didn't seem important with everything else that was going on."

"And he's tipping you a hundred thousand dollars? Who is he, the sultan of Brunei?"

"I never was too clear on how he made his money."

The news caught my father, as it had my mother and me, totally off guard. "I hardly know what to say, Lizzy," he said, taking a sip of Scotch as he sat back in his armchair in the library.

"Well, Sherman, you're going to have to see this thing for yourself," Mom said. "It certainly *looks* legitimate."

"You say you saved this man's life? How's that?"

"During a lesson."

"Why didn't you ever say anything to us?" he asked, swirling the ice around in his glass.

"She *said,* she didn't think it was *important,*" Mom said. "Can you imagine?"

"I guess we haven't been communicating with each other so well these last few months," Dad said.

"You can say that again," I conceded quietly. Finally, something on which we could agree.

That night Mom prepared marinated chicken thighs, sweet potatoes, and a Greek salad. As the level of the Merlot sank in the bottle, the three of us became unusually warm and fuzzy. I complimented Mom on the meal, asked Dad how his day at work went. We discussed the recent good news from the doctors, who were optimistic they'd gotten all of the cancer. It was amazing what a long way a hundred grand could go toward creating an atmosphere of generosity and tolerance. We could all look past our troubles to focus magnanimously on the here and now.

Dad said, "I think you should know, your mother and I are very proud of you." He cleared his throat then. I'm not positive, but he may have been getting a little choked up.

I'm not going to say it didn't feel good. If they'd ever used the word *proud* in relation to me before, I certainly didn't remember it.

And then, the hundred-thousand-dollar question: "Any thoughts about what you're going to do with the money?"

There were calls, calls, and more calls. Dad's financial advisers advised, but I was made to understand that a hundred grand was a mere chocolate bar compared to the sums they were used to dealing with.

In the end, I decided to keep things "liquid," as they say. The money relaxed me. Made me understand that it might actually be possible to take things one day at a time. I didn't have to become a doctor or a lawyer, or be the star in a Pete Laurey video. I also didn't have to be so hard on myself all the time.

When Mom was well enough to start bitching again, I gave Lynne a call.

"Come on back, Betty!" she said. She was vacuuming. "Your ticket's in the mail! You've got a place to stay! You won't need any money!" she yelled over the hum. She could be pretty anally compulsive when she got a bee in her bonnet.

"I want to be on your team for the Pole Pedal Paddle," I said.

"What did you say?"

"I said! Could you turn off the goddamn vacuum a second?"

"Yeah, sorry."

"That's better. I said, I want to be on your team for the Pole Pedal Paddle."

"Really? That's awesome! We were looking for a third to do the pedal leg."

"I'm your pedaler."

"I'll send you a ticket."

"Thanks, I've already got one."

"What happen, you win the lottery?"

"Sort of," I said. "Remember Cecil Black?"

"The guy who had the heart attack?"

"Right. I just got my tip in the mail."

"Enough for a plane ticket?"

"And then some."

With my forehead pressed against the tiny airplane window, I took in the jagged, snow-swept peaks of the Tetons. I could already feel the crisp, clean, pine-scented mountain air filling my lungs. A wave of excitement went through me, then relief. Those wild, wild mountains . . . I was coming home.

That night at Vista Grande, Lynne, Speed, and I threw back Cuervo margaritas on the rocks as we chowed on chimi-changas, enchiladas, chips, and guacamole.

Speed was looking a heck of a lot more prepped out than the last time I'd seen him. "What's with the Izod?" I asked.

"Birthday present from my woman," he said, clinking his glass on Lynne's.

"As long as he keeps me happy," she said.

"That some kinda threat, girl?"

"Damn right," she said, popping a chip in his mouth. "So, Betty, how does it feel to be back?"

"Awesome," I said, savoring the tart limyness of the drink.

"Hey, isn't that your ex?" Speed said, looking above our heads.

"I vowed no more waitresses," Lynne said.

"Not the waitress, you blanket chewer."

"*Excuse* me?" she asked, bursting into laughter.

"I think you mean carpet muncher," I corrected.

We were all laughing merrily away when Max Wright came up to the table. "Lynne, Harlin, Betty, long time no see."

"What are you talking about, we saw you three days ago," Lynne said.

"I meant Betty," he said.

"So I guess it really is over between us," Lynne said.

"Yes, Lynne, and I want you to quit stalking me."

"So you *have* been getting my letters."

"What's that you've been spraying them with, Jean Naté?"

"All right, that's enough, you two, or someone's going to get their hide tanned," Speed said.

"So how was New Canaan?" he asked.

"Still quaint as hell," I said.

He nodded and sucked in his cheeks, exchanging a meaningful glance with Lynne.

"What?" I asked.

"Nothing," Lynne said.

"Lynne told me about what happened with Jack."

"We don't mention that name around here anymore by the way," Lynne said.

"When I called your house and told your mother I was a friend from Jackson, she hung up on me. I figured there had to be a reason. I just wanted to see how you were doing."

"Wow, Doc, that's pretty above and beyond," I said.

Here was a guy who took caregiving seriously, who wasn't a cheater, and who looked like Jake Gyllenhaal to boot. A *doctor* no less. Maybe I was ready for something or someone a bit more stable? Not that he was stepping up to the plate exactly . . .

"By the way, we need a third for the ski leg of the Pole Pedal Paddle. You think you could be good to go by next Saturday?"

Then again, he wasn't exactly backing down.

"You're damn right she's going to be good to go," Lynne said. "Too bad she's riding for team *Speed*."

"Would a chicken-fried steak sweeten the deal?" he asked.

Definitely taking a swing at the ball.

I shrugged and said, "Sorry, I gotta do what my girl says."

Raising her glass, Lynne said, "To Betty."

"All right, since you're so determined to be on the losing team—"

"*Losing* team?" Lynne interrupted.

"Easy there, amigo," Speed said.

"I'm sorry, I don't even know what that word *means*," I said, the way only someone who's lost and lived could.

"I've always found you learn more from losing than you do from winning," Max said, grinning. "Perhaps you'd like to ski the pass with me Monday to soften the blow?"

One thing's for sure, if you let your *fear* of losing cripple you, then you might as well make "Loser" your middle name. Which is why I went into mountain mode when I replied, "You're on."

acknowledgments

My love affair with Jackson, Wyoming, would never have begun (or continued) without the enduring friendship and unparalleled hospitality of Anne Ladd, Len, Madeline and Reed Carlman, Beedee, Ted, Sr., Ted, Jr., and Laura Ladd. Skiing is an expensive sport into which one is preferably introduced early in life. I owe my own timely inauguration and subsequent immersion to the considerable expense (financial and otherwise) of my parents, Donald and Rina McCouch. For leading me up and down more mountains than I can count and teaching me how to get it right, I owe a great debt of gratitude to Chris Rogers, Max and Julie Gregoric, Hess Mirghavami, Peter Barker, Marina MacDonald, and Cheryl Carol Merrill. Simon Green, Bruce Tracy, and Adam Korn deserve medals for their good humor, insight, and patience during the writing of this book. I am especially grateful to my husband, Stephen Angus MacGillivray, whose encouragement and double baby duty enabled me to write.

about the author

HANNAH McCOUCH is the author of the novel *Girl Cook*. She grew up in New York and Connecticut, before moving to Alta, Utah, and Jackson Hole, Wyoming, where she worked as a ski instructor and cocktail waitress. Her writing has appeared in numerous publications including *Cosmopolitan*, *Glamour*, and *Blue* magazines. A graduate of Hamilton College, Le Cordon Bleu, and Columbia University's M.F.A. Writing Division, she now lives in New York City with her husband and daughter.

This book was set in Quadraat Sans, a typeface designed by Fred Smeijers. His first Quadraat typeface was serifed, and he successfully adapted it to a sans version without sacrificing its lively and humane character. Quadraat Sans has display qualities yet it is efficient, making it equally suitable for texts. Fred Smeijers (born 1961) was educated in typography and graphic design at the Arnhem Academy of Art and Design. He has been designing typefaces since the 1980s.